D1112713

The Devil's Triangle

Other Novels by Howard Owen

Littlejohn
Fat Lightning
Answers to Lucky
The Measured Man
Harry and Ruth
The Rail
Turn Signal
Rock of Ages
The Reckoning

Willie Black Series

Oregon Hill
The Philadelphia Quarry
Parker Field
The Bottom
Grace

The Devil's Triangle

HOWARD OWEN

The Permanent Press
Sag Harbor, NY 11963

For information, address:
The Permanent Press
4170 Noyac Road
Sag Harbor, NY 11963
www.thepermanentpress.com

Library of Congress Cataloging-in-Publication Data
Owen, Howard, author.
The devil's triangle / Howard Owen.
Sag Harbor, NY : Permanent Press, [2017]
ISBN 978-1-57962-499-6
1. Reporters and reporting—Fiction. 2. Murder—Investigation—Fiction. 3. Richmond (Va.)—Fiction. 4. Mystery fiction.

PS3565.W552 D48 2017
813'.54—dc23 2017008730

Printed in the United States of America

As always, to Karen

CHAPTER ONE

April 8, 2016

In the flaming hell that used to be one of my watering holes, last call came about eight hours early.

You don't really expect a twin-engine Beechcraft to crash through the plate-class window during happy hour.

The Hispanic guy coming out of the 7-Eleven across the street said he heard it, loud at first and then louder, then right on top of him. When I quoted him as saying it sounded like a freight train, Sally Velez accused me of making shit up.

Five thirty on a Friday afternoon is usually the calm before the storm on the night cops beat. Happy hour is when the folks who eventually go through the seven stages of drunkenness (sober, happy, happier, tipsy, unhappy, unhappier, and homicidal) are just getting started. The construction worker who's buying his buddies a round at five thirty probably won't be employing his weapon of choice until midnight or so.

This one jumped the gun. Our first inkling was on Twitter, of course. Who the hell needs police radios anymore?

"Plane crash. Peeps dead. Sheperd & Patterson."

The tweeter meant Sheppard Street. I knew where it was and was out the door in what might have been record time for a fifty-something confirmed smoker. Chip Grooms caught up with me and hopped in at the parking-deck gate as I was screeching onto the street. Even though the bean counters would rather have reporters take the pictures too, it's good to have a real photographer along for the really big stuff so we can properly record the mayhem.

The cops already had blocked off everything within a city block by the time we got there. We had to park almost to the Virginia Museum. Even from there, you could see the black smoke. The sun, not quite down to tree level yet, was a malevolent red ball.

Everybody enjoying this fine April afternoon at the other beer dispensaries nearby was out gawking, and the police were having a hard time keeping them back.

I spotted Gillespie, who let Grooms and me through the yellow tape. I told him I owed him a dozen from the Sugar Shack. He didn't seem averse to the offer.

A few seconds after we slipped inside the lines, I wasn't so sure Gillespie had done me a favor.

I've seen dead people, lots of dead people. Most of them have been shot, usually at close range, usually by a drug colleague or a close family member. I've been to a few executions and seen the human light go out firsthand.

I'd never seen a plane crash, though, or its aftermath. There are some things that you'd be advised to leave off the bucket list, trust me.

The smell was what hit me first. Burned human flesh is a pretty good appetite suppressant. The space where Dark Star had been, along with the dry cleaners next door, was a smoking ruin, with the last of the fires—I guess from the plane's fuel—still being extinguished. The plane, as it came in, must have clipped off the top of the 7-Eleven's sign, leaving a jagged top that read "Oh Thank Heaven." Who says God doesn't have a sense of humor? Other commercial establishments, and a couple of nearby houses, had suffered various degrees of damage.

The EMTs were trying to do some good, but you could see they were having a hard time distinguishing among the dead, the dying, and the salvageable.

A person, who might have been twenty-one or sixty-five, was being cared for as best they could. I think it was a woman. She was screaming, but it came out weak, like her vocal cords had maybe been cooked along with the rest of the body. I could hear the tremor in the young rescue worker's voice as he lied and said it was going to be all right. Her hair and clothes had all been burned off, and what was underneath was not going to be worth saving. I could have told the guy that, but he probably already knew.

There was a blackened, still smoldering thing lying just off the sidewalk. I was on top of it before I realized it used to be somebody's arm.

Grooms has covered a lot of car wrecks, I'm sure, but he looked like I felt. We each just wanted to go somewhere and puke.

I found Larry Doby Jones, our chief of police, standing half a block from the carnage. The smoke was like a toxic fog around us, and he kept swiping his hand in front of his face, like he could brush it, and the smell, away.

"Who the hell let you in here?" he greeted me. Even his dislike for me, though, couldn't outweigh the enormity of the moment. In a minute or so, he was telling me more than he usually does, which is nothing. I guess there was some kind of shared foxhole shit going on there. It would wear off, I was sure, and L.D. soon would be calling me a "big-nosed, meddling son of a bitch" again, like old times.

He didn't make me leave, and I did have a better vantage point than the TV contingent, which smelled blood and was barely being restrained like a pack of baying hounds behind the aforementioned yellow tape.

It was after eight by the time I had enough information to go back and write my story. I would have preferred to have taken a shower first. I wondered if I'd ever get the smell of smoke and death off me. A Camel would have helped my general sanity, but there was too much fuel spilled that hadn't burned up.

Grooms had been sending photos back from his digital camera, and I'd been calling Sally Velez every half hour so she could feed the online beast. I'd just rounded up Grooms and was about to head back when I saw a familiar face through the gloom, outlined by the smoldering ruins of a perfectly good bar.

Kate looked a little frantic. Well, a lot frantic. She had somehow gotten inside police lines and seemed to be grilling a noncooperative flatfoot about something.

I touched her. She spun around. I had never seen Kate Ellis, my third ex-wife, look so out of control. I'd seen her lose her temper plenty of times, had been the match that set off her powder keg on more than one occasion, but this was different. I wasn't sure at first if she even knew me. She seemed ready to hit the first thing she saw. She did land one pretty good punch to my chest before I restrained her. And then she broke down.

"Greg's dead. They're all dead," she said. She was sobbing. Kate doesn't sob—at least, not in my presence. But she was bawling now. "Every goddamn one of them. Dead!"

Then she screamed. Occasionally, as the hellish afternoon wore on, people looking for a loved one would come rushing up, see what a plane crash can do to a bar, and lose it. This time, it was Kate's turn.

"Greg! Greg!"

I looked around for him, but then I knew what she meant.

It took a little while to get to the hard, cold facts, but finally she did.

They hadn't released the names of any of the victims yet and wouldn't until sometime after our Saturday deadline. But Kate knew who was there, or at least some of them.

The partners at Bartley, Bowman and Bush, Kate's old firm, always did happy hour on Fridays, after a busy week of over-billing clients. They often invited some of the other attorneys to join them. Of late, they had been getting happy at Dark Star, the joint that was now mostly cinders in front of us.

Kate had left BB&B a couple of years ago for the lucrative world of ambulance chasing and occasional conscience-salving pro bono work as the associate of Marcus Green, but she still had friends there. One of them had called her, an hour after the crash, to tell her that many of her former associates were inside when the plane hit.

One of the lawyers invited to join the partners was Greg Ellis, my ex-wife's most recent husband. Yes, they were separated, but they were, as they say, "trying to work it out."

"He's in there," she said. She made a move toward the ruins, apparently not for the first time, from what the cop told me as he helped me restrain her.

I assured Kate that whoever or whatever was inside had now been removed by the EMTs. The police, as she knew, would be contacting her as soon as they could get around to notifying the next of kin. I promised to help her check with the local hospitals.

I asked her where Grace was. She said she had left their daughter, now three years old, in the care of Marcus Green.

"Greg might be OK," I told her. It was as optimistic as I could be without lying like a dog. "Some of them were."

Eventually, with Chip Grooms's help, I got her back to our car, and we drove her to the offices of Green and Ellis on

Franklin Street. I walked her in and handed her off to Marcus. I asked her if she had somewhere to stay, and she gave me a strange look and said she'd be staying at home, of course. I wondered silently if that was a good idea but left it at that.

Everyone who'd ever worked at the paper seemed to be in the newsroom. It was some kind of a record for a Friday night in our recent, dystopian march to obsolescence, marked by layoffs, furloughs, and shortened hours. I saw a couple of people who had been canned in the last two years working the phones for a company that had turned them out in their late fifties to try their luck in the job market. Unrequited love is a terrible thing. Hell, if they fired me, I'd probably do the same thing—come back like a dumbass to help my former coworkers deal with a once-in-a-lifetime disaster. Yeah, part of it goes beyond benevolence. We're hooked on tragedy.

The numbers would change over the next few days, as some of the hopeless gave up hope, but the original tally, the one that we ran in Saturday's paper, was twenty-two dead and another twenty-nine injured. The block looked like pictures I've seen of London during the Blitz.

"Man," I heard Ray Long say. "The Devil's Triangle."

Nobody much has called it that for a while. The people who had turned the Tiki, the Ritz, and the Rainbow Room, whose denizens used to bedevil Richmond's image protectors and terrorize the citizenry, into a more Yuppified neighborhood certainly didn't want the name to stick. They went to great lengths to ensure that it was now part of the Museum District, seeing how it was a stone's throw away from the Virginia Museum and the Virginia Historical Society. Old-timers, though, still sometimes use the fallen-from-grace name. We don't let go of old shit very easily in Richmond. Hell, some of us haven't abandoned the Civil War yet.

Dark Star, the place that was destroyed, chock-full of patrons when the plane hit, had been a favorite of mine for some time. It had changed names, but I'm a creature of habit. Hell, I spent a few dollars there on Saint Patrick's Day with Abe Custalow, Andy Peroni, and R.P. McGonnigal. We all agreed that we each had at least some Irish lineage, as if the lack of same would have kept us from celebrating, any more than a dearth of Hispanic blood keeps us from sucking down margaritas on Cinco de Mayo.

I had no doubt that some of those who died or would mercifully expire later from burns had sat elbow to elbow with me at the bar on occasion. It did make it seem more personal.

Some of the more grizzled among us exchanged stories about the 1970s and early '80s, when the Triangle was going strong. I was still in college when the old places started to fall by the wayside, but Bootie Carmichael could remember when he had an apartment on Kensington and could call the Rainbow to have a boy on a bicycle deliver a couple of six-packs when Bootie was either too lazy or too incapacitated to make the two-block walk.

"I'd always give him one of the beers for a tip," Bootie said. "Hell, the kid was probably at least fourteen."

"Tell me again," Sarah Goodnight said to me, low enough that Bootie probably couldn't hear her, "why I'm supposed to miss the good old days."

We ran a few of the names, confirmed from family members. Among them was Gregory Watts Ellis. Before we locked up the last edition, we also had nailed down the names of the two partners at BB&B who were killed, plus the other partner and two other associates who might by then have considered death a favor. Being some of the higher-ranking and higher-paid lawyers in town, they were the lede to my story.

I called Kate's home for the third time. The house is so big that she and Greg both continued to live there after their separation. This time, a man answered. I recognized his voice.

Kate's father. I was relieved that she had had the presence of mind to call someone. I had visions of her sitting there, going crazy, while the phone rang off the hook.

"Ah, yes. Willie," Cade Longstreet said. He said "Willie" with approximately the same warmth with which he might have said "Ebola."

"So good of you to call."

Even before Kate and I broke up, I never really felt the love from Kate's family. They had brought their daughter up to know better than to marry a journalist. Our breakup was not met with wailing and gnashing of teeth.

I kept it short. I was mainly making sure that Kate was OK, or as OK as somebody can be when her husband has recently been incinerated.

"Yes, yes," Cade said. "Kate's fine. She's resting now. I'll tell her you called."

The old bastard acted like I was calling his daughter to ask her out, now that she was free. Well, disaster doesn't exactly bring out our best natures. I wished him the best and hung up. Actually I just hung up.

What we couldn't find out was who the hell piloted the plane. There understandably wasn't much left of him. There also wasn't any record of a plane like the one that crashed being anywhere in the Richmond area. The aviation folks said it just seemed to come out of nowhere.

We were assured that we would be informed of the pilot's identity and get some idea of what the hell he was doing flying into a crowded eatery, all in good time.

In the meantime, of course, everybody had their own opinions. Most people in our town who have opinions seem averse to keeping them to themselves. They prefer to post them on the newspaper's website, where they try to outdo each other. ("You think you've got some crazy ideas? I'll show you crazy!")

The primary story line was that the pilot was a terrorist, bent on raining destruction on our fair city.

"It's just like 9-11," one of them typed. "Muslum extremists. Ought to round 'em all up and send 'em back to Crapistan."

He had, last time I looked, 598 "likes" and more snarling "amens" than I could get around to reading.

The TV folk picked up on the terrorist thing, once they got their teeth into it. They used slightly less offensive language than the online Yosemite Sams, but the thrust was the same. You can put question marks on just about anything and turn the ridiculous into a plausible theory.

"Was the tragic air disaster in Richmond today the work of foreign terrorists?" wondered one of the local anchors, standing out there amid the wreckage and trying to breathe through his mouth. Might just as well have said, "The towelheads did it. Let's get 'em."

Even in the newsroom, the conjecture was drifting toward intentional assault by individuals with funny last names.

"Just like Richmond," Enos Jackson said. "New York City gets 767s. We get a damn twin-engine Beechcraft."

It was suggested by one of our all-knowing online contributors that perhaps the pilot was an angry African American bent on destroying all the Confederate monuments a few blocks away. That got its own likes and follow-up mouth foaming.

I rarely respond on our online site, but this time I made an exception. I noted that the half of Richmond that is African American has had many opportunities to rid us of our paeans to the Lost Cause without resorting to an airplane. I also noted that the structures on Monument Avenue would be a hell of a lot easier to hit than a pitiful little eatery so packed in by other buildings that the pilot couldn't help but have some major collateral damage. In other words, Robert E. Lee, Stonewall Jackson, Jeb Stuart, and Jeff Davis were easy targets. You probably could spot their statues from three miles up. How does a pilot get so lost that he plows into a congested block of eateries and small shopkeepers instead?

All logic got me was some scorching retorts, mostly claiming that, as usual, the liberal media was trying to do a cover-up. Liberal? Jesus, don't these guys read our editorial pages? A couple of the kind-hearted bastards even made note of my mixed-race heritage.

"How can we trust a black guy named Black to tell the truth?" one of them typed. I heeded Sally Velez's advice and did not contribute further to our community forum.

Our publisher, Rita Dominick, sent word via Mal Wheelwright that we should address all the whack-job theories in our stories. I flat refused. Wheelie's the editor, but I'm not going to put something in print that neither he nor I believe for a second.

"Evolution is a theory," I told Wheelie. "Relativity is a theory. This is just bullshit."

Without agreeing with me, he assigned Mark Baer to do a sidebar on the ponderings of lunatics. Against my sage advice, they ran it on A1, right below my main story. Not to be outdone by the TV geniuses, the headline read: Terrorism behind attack? The subhead read: Racial motivation also suggested.

It's midnight now. Already we've learned that some brave souls have defaced the nearest mosque they could find.

Maybe the guy blaming the "Muslins" or the one who thought somebody wanted to take out the Lee Monument and missed was right. Hell, I don't know.

I just know how many times I've seen the obvious answer turn out to be the wrong one.

"Let me check around," I tell Wheelie.

"I never doubted you would," he says. "Just keep an open mind."

If I do, I tell him, it might be unique in the city of Richmond.

CHAPTER TWO

Saturday

Richmonders can rest easy.

It appears that the holy city is not on the ISIS hit list. This probably does not make the still-living victims or the dead's next of kin feel any better, but it's about the closest thing to good news we have right now.

Early this morning, a man in Topping, over on the Middle Peninsula, called the authorities. He'd come in late last night from fishing on the bay and then drinking in Kilmarnock. Today he was going to take a couple of his fishing/drinking buddies up in his private plane. If you guessed that it was a twin-engine Beechcraft, you win a free year's viewership on the paper's website. Oh, wait, it's already free.

The only problem was, the plane wasn't there. When he drove over to the mom-and-pop air strip where he keeps—or, kept—it, it wasn't there. Since the guy was pretty sure the plane hadn't flown itself, he could come up with only one other possibility.

A guy had been renting from him, staying out in a shack out back of the big house. The guy was gone. The plane was gone. The guy didn't have a pilot's license, the plane's owner said, but he had had one at one time and did know how to fly. He had, the owner admitted, flown the now-departed Bay Beauty on a couple of occasions.

His name was David Biggio. Once the cops had a name, it wasn't that hard to track down some much-needed information. Biggio had lived in Topping for about seven years. Before that, information was sketchy. A quick check in our electronic files, though, showed that he had lived in Richmond as late as 2007. That's when he was arrested for stalking his former wife, from whom he was divorced the year before.

It seemed, from the files, that he got away with a suspended sentence. After that, nothing for the last nine years.

And, blowing a hole in the deranged-black-racist theories, Mr. Biggio appears to have been white.

They were pretty sure Mr. DNA soon would identify David Biggio as the man who either accidentally or intentionally killed twenty-two people, with a few more likely to join the list in the near future.

We learned all that at the chief's press conference, called at the ungodly hour of nine A.M. Peachy Love phoned me at home to tell me about it, otherwise I might have missed it. The big dog for our police department, Larry Doby Jones, doesn't mind a bit if I'm not as informed as the paper's night cops reporter should be.

L.D. was in his element, holding court before not only the local news media but also a host of out-of-towners, from Washington, New York, and other places where they usually write us off as hopeless provincials. The mayor managed to get his butt up on the podium, too, looking somber. He said a few words about "our city's darkest day," maybe forgetting the time the Confederate troops accidentally burned the place to the ground in their haste to flee the approaching Union army.

It must have been a disappointment to them both when the out-of-town newshounds disappeared faster than a ten-dollar bill at Starbucks as it became clear that the guy who crashed his plane into Dark Star was a homeboy and not some nut from Fuck-me-deadistan. He might have been a terrorist, but he was our terrorist, by God, which made his charred remains a bit less sexy, six-o'clock-newswise. Instead of an orange alert, we have some white guy who crashed a plane into a packed bar.

And, it is highly possible, given the fact that Mr. Biggio apparently had not been apprehended for any other criminal activity since he quit stalking his ex-wife, that it was a sheer accident, the kind that makes people question their religious beliefs.

"God tests us," I heard a preacher say last night when one of the more idiotic of the local TV stations found one willing to explain the inexplicable, why bad things happen to good people and all that shit.

If yesterday was a test, I think I'm about ready to drop this course. Sam McNish, who has gotten Cindy and me to come to his makeshift church a few times after I helped save his ass last year, will be appalled to find out that my faith, microscopic mustard seed that it was, has shrunk to subatomic levels.

Mark Baer was there. He said he happened to be in the newsroom at seven forty-five A.M. when the e-mail message about the pilot's identity came in.

I asked him why he didn't call me at home. He said he didn't want to wake me. He asked me how I found out about the press conference. He didn't seem all that happy to see me there. He just went from A1 lede story on Sunday morning to maybe a sidebar. Mark lives to be above the fold on A1.

I suggested to Baer that he might go back to the scene for some second-day reaction quotes. He gave me a sour look and walked away.

I stop by to see Peggy on the way in to work. My mother, now in her seventy-fourth year, does not seem to be slowing down. OK; maybe she's smoking a little less pot than she did ten years ago, but her energy level when she's stoned is higher than most people's when they're clean and sober. Today, in the morning chill, she's hanging sheets and various clothing on the line in her backyard. I remind her that I bought her a washer and dryer five years ago, and that she doesn't need to be freezing her butt off out here with clothespins in her mouth.

She spits one out into her free hand and says she needs to keep moving.

"I'm like a shark," she says. "If I sit still, I'm a goner. Besides, they smell better when you dry 'em in God's own air."

I decline to argue further. Hell, she's in better shape than I am despite a handicap of eighteen years.

Andi and young William, my daughter and grandson, are still living with Peggy, as is the ever-wandering Awesome Dude, who seems to spend more time in the English basement these days and less roaming through the homeless shelters, parks, and hobo jungles that were his natural habitat before Peggy took him in.

I stay long enough for a cup of coffee and to get the latest on Andi's long and winding academic career. I am pleased to say that the end is in sight. A degree seems to be in the works next month, a mere nine years after Andi graduated from high school. It's in sociology, but a journalism major has no right to cast aspersions on anyone's chosen field. There might actually be jobs available in sociology in the future.

The little rental on Oregon Hill is a far cry from what Andi could enjoy if she would yield to the pleading of William's father, Thomas Jefferson Blandford V, but my daughter's a romantic fool who thinks you shouldn't marry a guy just because he knocked you up, even if he is rich as Croesus.

"Dad," she told me the last time I gently broached the subject of common sense versus the heart, "if I'm going to spend the rest of my life with him, I ought to at least love the son of a bitch."

She comes by her romantic tendencies naturally. I've often fallen in love. I have three divorces to prove it. But I'm not afraid to get right back on that horse, although I'm not sure the lovely Cindy Peroni would appreciate the equine analogy.

The newsroom is in post-storm mode when I get in at eleven thirty, a good three hours before my work day is supposed to start. Many of my compatriots, like me, were there even after the city edition rolled. We were trying to make sense out of the senseless and figure out where we go from here.

Then, like all good journalists at the end of a day full of excitement and other people's tragedy, we went over to Penny Lane and tried to drink ourselves into a coma.

So far only a few of my coworkers have straggled in for Day Two. Baer's there, of course. He's talking with Sarah Goodnight over in the corner. When he sees me, he gives me a quick glance and walks away in what looks suspiciously like a huff.

"Is your boyfriend miffed at me?" I ask her.

"If you reference him, me, and 'boyfriend' in the same sentence again, I will punch you squarely in the balls."

I take a short step back and compliment her on her improved taste in men.

"He's just pissed that he didn't get to do the press conference story," she goes on. "He said he thought he was doing you a favor, by not waking you. We all know how much you senior citizens need your sleep."

Anytime Mark Baer claims he's doing me a favor, my bullshit detector activates.

As for the snarky remark about stamina, I ask Sarah who helped whom out of Penny Lane at closing time last night.

"Touché," she concedes.

I ask her if any other tidbits have surfaced. This story is going to be with us for a month, I feel certain. We're just in the hunting and gathering mode right now.

"I'm trying to get in touch with the ex-wife, but she seems to have disappeared."

I note that having your former husband turn into a stalker probably would make her want to go low profile.

We've only had a couple of hours to start putting the pieces together, but Sarah already has checked all records and determined that David Biggio's wife is not on any list of taxpayers, car owners, or other city residents from whom the city can wrest a few dollars come tax time. She's starting to work the nearby counties now.

"Nothing I can dig up on Google either," she says.

Her name, at the time of the stalking incident, was Louisa Biggio.

"She might have gone back to her maiden name," I suggest, but Sarah's already checked that out and come away with nothing.

I ask about the guy who owned the plane. About all I know after the press conference is that he lives in Topping, a dot on the map out near the Chesapeake, and that his name is James Ware.

Sarah checks her notes.

"Chopper Ware," she says. "That's what they call him."

I ask her how she found out that tidbit.

She shrugs.

"Just called around to a few places. He owns a hardware store out there. Quite the local character, from what I gather. Somebody said he broke his arm last year falling off a barstool."

I ask Sarah what's wrong with falling off a barstool and make a mental note that my job soon will demand that I take a trip down to the bay, perhaps stopping off at Lowery's in Tappahannock for some fried shrimp. Tappahannock isn't directly on the way to Topping, but nobody above my pay grade around here knows shit about Virginia once you get outside what they call the core circulation area, so who'll be the wiser?

And speaking of my superiors, I am soon made aware of our publisher's presence. I don't know what kind of perfume Rita Dominick uses, but I can often smell her before I see her. It isn't an unpleasant scent, but there's just so damn much of it.

"How's it going?" she asks, innocently enough. She is more or less on speaking terms with me these days despite our occasional contretemps. This is only a temporary truce, I am sure.

Ms. Dominick hadn't expected to be here this long. She was, it is commonly known, brought in to thin the herd so that our chain could sell us and gain some much-needed cash to pay off the rest of their ill-conceived debts. Then she would move on to pillage somebody else's paper. Well, the herd is anorexic. Mission accomplished. But nobody wants us. We're like the ugly baby everybody passes over at the orphanage.

It could be worse. A friend at a slightly smaller paper that was just bought by the Friedman chain that nearly bought us told me last week that they'd laid off the copy desk.

The hatchet man brought in by Friedman told the staff that a paper their size didn't need a copy desk.

Ray Long, who has been saving people's asses for forty years by catching everything from misplaced commas to libelous screwups, went kind of pale when I relayed that gem to him.

"My life," he said, "apparently has been a waste. Who needs facts? Who needs subjects and verbs to agree?"

Sarah brings our publisher up to speed on the pilot's ex-wife and Chopper Ware. Feeling the need to say something that will make her sound like a cross between Donald Trump and a high-school football coach, Ms. Dominick tells her to "get off your butt and find that woman. I expect to see that in tomorrow's paper.

"And you," she says, turning my way. "Get your ass down there and find out what you can about this nutcase. Find that guy whose plane he crashed."

She gets up on a chair and then on a desk. She seems about as close to losing her shit as I've seen her, but I know it's all for effect.

"People!" she says, getting the attention of the dozen of us who have now clocked in. "This is the biggest story you might ever cover. We're going to want everybody on this 24/7! This is our story!"

Satisfied that she has put the fear of God in her newsroom, she climbs down from the desk, perhaps wishing she had worn a slightly longer skirt. As soon as the elevator doors close behind her, her minions—most of whom are copy editors or sports desk guys who will have little to do with the execution of this story—look at one another and silently wish, for the umpteenth time, that they could win the lottery and go climb on Rita Dominick's desk.

Wheelie comes in half an hour later. Our editor gives us a toned-down version of the publisher's pep talk. He has obviously already been up to her office and been told to keep the heat on. Wheelie knows that, slackers though we may be when the day-to-day crap is involved, we don't need anybody to go all Vince Lombardi on us when a story this big hits.

"Just do what you need to do to get it right," he tells Sarah, Baer, and me, plus anyone else in listening range. "I don't need to tell you that."

One thing I'll say for Ms. Dominick. She makes everybody appreciate Wheelie's management style.

I tell Sarah that I'll see what I can find out about Louisa Biggio and Chopper Ware as soon as I write something off the press conference, mostly for our website. Read it for free right now or buy a paper tomorrow morning? Tough choice for our audience.

I call Cindy, who is sharing living quarters with Custalow and me. That's working out so far, by the way. Actually better than working out. Abe and I occasionally have a home-cooked meal that doesn't involve the microwave. Also housekeeping has taken a decided turn for the better. It isn't that she cleans up after us. It's more like she expects us to clean up after ourselves. The last time Kate, my ex and our landlady, made one of her unannounced visits to ensure that I'm not smoking indoors or otherwise ruining the place's resale value, she e-mailed me later to express her delight in the relative cleanliness of our little Prestwould ménage à trois.

"It wasn't that tidy when I was living there," she wrote.

"Wonder why?" I responded.

Cindy hasn't seen much of me the last couple of days. She was working on a term paper yesterday and was too tired to come out with our after-work crowd to try to drink Penny Lane dry. And she was still asleep when I got my heads-up call about this morning's press conference. If things go well, my live-in sweetie and my daughter will both graduate this May. Talk about a win-win. No more tuition and fees, plus the likelihood that Custalow and I will have a third party paying rent sometime soon.

"So you've got a full day today," she says when I call. "I don't guess you'll be able to run home for dinner."

I tell her I'll try, but she knows how little success I usually have when I try.

"Well, maybe I'll come down and say hi at some point. Lisa and Mary Anne wanted me to go to a movie with them this evening, if you're pretty sure you can't get away."

I tell her to have fun and try not to get picked up.

"Or at least," I add, "don't bring him home. The neighbors will talk."

She laughs.

"Like they aren't already."

Yeah. The Prestwould can be a pretty small place, a little village where everybody knows what everybody else is doing, or at least thinks they do. The better class of neighbor, like Clara Westbrook, knows there's nothing kinky going on on the sixth floor. Or, if they do suspect, they're too well-mannered to mention it. Others, like the ever-suspicious Feldman, broadcast rumors like a sneeze spreads germs. He loves to ask me, in a voice dripping with insinuation, how "things" are going. When I ask him what "things" he's talking about, he just smirks. Feldman is, unfortunately, too old to slap.

"I still can't get over Kate's husband being one of the ones who died," Cindy says. "Have you talked to her?"

I tell her about running into Kate at the site.

"Oh, my god," she says. "That must have been awful."

I mention calling last night to make sure she was OK.

There is a slight pause, and then Cindy says that Kate probably has family to help her get through it.

I can read the slight pause like a seventy-two-point headline: It isn't your job to make sure your ex-wife is coping with the death of her husband, whom she probably was going to divorce anyhow, just like she did you.

Cindy and Kate have met, and neither tried to claw the other's eyes out. There is, though, a bit of tension there. It happens when you move in with a guy who's renting the place from his ex-wife.

I concede that Kate indeed does have family with her, but I don't promise that I won't check up on her again. I just won't mention it if I do.

WE GET the names of almost all the victims for the Sunday paper. Various staffers track down next of kin and get the obligatory information and quotes about the departed. There were, in addition to the heart and soul of BB&B, two teachers, an accountant, two couples still in college, and several working-class stiffs from the neighborhood. We were able to get photographs of most of them.

Mostly when you go tromping through other people's tragedies, they are polite, probably because they're still in shock and want to validate their loss by getting some information in print about their loved ones.

Occasionally someone gets angry and tells you to go fuck yourself, but that's usually a cousin who thinks he's protecting the privacy of the survivor. Hell, if somebody called me at a time like this, I might also suggest sexual self-gratification.

As for the "why?"—we're still working on that. Beyond assuring our uneasy readers that this was not a mini 9/11 or the work of angry black people, we're still in the head-scratching phase.

We don't know much about David Biggio either. Neither Sarah nor I have been able to unearth his former wife yet, but I have a few calls out. You don't live in a city your whole life and not develop some contacts. One of them will come through. They always do. Hopefully this will happen before impatience impels Ms. Dominick to climb up on a desk again.

That is a sight no one should have to endure twice.

CHAPTER THREE

Sunday

Jumpin' Jimmy Deacon is no slave to the clock.

Five A.M., five P.M., it's all the same to Jumpin' Jimmy. The fact that he probably doesn't sleep is, I'm sure, a contributing factor.

When I started trolling for some evidence of David Biggio's former wife, something clicked. At the time when he was arrested for stalking back in '07, his ex-wife was living at a place on Crenshaw. I remembered that Jimmy Deacon lived on the same block. So I left a message on Jumpin' Jimmy's phone late yesterday afternoon. I had thrown out lures everywhere, calling or e-mailing a dozen other people who might have had some contact with Biggio's former wife. Jimmy was the one who bit.

He called this morning. At five fifteen. I recognized the voice right away.

"Hey, Hoss, what can I do you for?" he said loud enough for Cindy, now awake like me, to mouth, "What the hell?"

I mouthed back, "Jumpin' Jimmy." She rolled her eyes and rolled back over.

Well, he definitely woke me up like a double espresso. Most people don't call you before sunup unless they have bad news to impart. When my heartbeat began to drop below 150 a minute, I stifled my first instinct, which was to threaten to twist Jimmy's neck off. I needed information.

"Sorry I didn't get back to you quicker," he said. "But Jumpin' Jimmy's been busy as a one-legged man in a butt-kicking contest. The Squirrels are back."

Jimmy Deacon has worked for three different minor-league baseball operations here, pretty much straight through since he was a teenager. It's what he does. Another season is starting, and Jimmy's on it, helping the Flying Squirrels' maintenance crew, ticket sales staff, or filling in anywhere else he's needed.

He's in his seventies now, with the energy and intellectual level of a hamster on a treadmill.

But he knows half the town. He's the kind of guy who makes it his business to know your business, whether it's any of his business or not. And he's a genius at remembering names, if nothing else. His encyclopedic knowledge of old Richmond baseball players helped me get on A1, sell a few papers, and keep my corporate masters temporarily happy a few years back.

"Yeah, yeah. Louisa and David Biggio. They were neighbors of mine. Jumpin' Jimmy didn't know 'em all that good, but they lived right up the street. He was kinda nutty."

Having Jimmy Deacon judge you "nutty" is like being called intolerant by the KKK.

I asked Jimmy if he had any idea where an enterprising reporter might find Louisa Biggio.

"Oh, yeah. I had to think about it for a minute, but then I remembered. She got married again. This fella moved into their apartment, after the husband left. First thing I know, I hear they're married."

I asked, fingers crossed, if he remembered the guy's name.

"Yeah, yeah. Jumpin' Jimmy never forgets a name. It was Klassen. Bobby Klassen."

He spelled it out for me.

"I heard they bought a place somewhere not far from Crenshaw, in the Museum District."

Jimmy is not a regular reader of my paper. When I told him that David Biggio was almost certainly the one who piloted the plane that demolished Dark Star and carried off many of its patrons, he told me to "get the fuck outta here."

"That doesn't really surprise me though," he said. "He seemed like the kind of fella that might do something like that."

I thank Jimmy for his time and tell him we need to get together and have a drink.

"Yeah, yeah," he says. "I'll call you."

I gently suggest that he do it sometime when the sun is shining.

"Oh, yeah," Jimmy says, just before I hang up, "there was a kid."

"A kid?"

"Yeah. Louisa, she had a little girl. She was a toddler when they split up, I think."

Now more or less wide awake, I roll out of bed, reluctantly leaving the warmth of my sweetie, now stacking zees again and snoring adorably.

I always keep a pen on the bedside table. A surprising number of people seem to think that, like Jumpin' Jimmy, I never sleep and thus am always available for calls, day or night.

So with Bobby Klassen's name scribbled on a sheet of notepad, I stumble into the den and start searching.

There is, praise God and Switchboard.com, a Robert Klassen who lives not three blocks from the old Crenshaw address. Looking it up on Google Maps, I am struck by the fact that the house where I am assuming the former Louisa Biggio, and perhaps her daughter, lives is about five blocks from the smoking ruins of Dark Star.

Why David Biggio's ex hasn't come forward already for her fifteen minutes of fame is a question I hope to have answered soon. Maybe she's one of those rare people who doesn't want nosy-ass reporters or camera crews stomping all over the flowers in her front yard.

You might call somebody with a hot tip before sunup, but you sure as hell don't make contact with a possible and likely uncooperative source at such an ungodly hour. I'm thinking sometime after noon might be a good idea. There is the outside chance that Richmond's finest will get in touch with her before then, but I doubt it. Plus, that Cindy-scented bed is calling my name. Time for a Willie wake-up call.

We are giving Sam McNish's makeshift church a miss this morning and opting to worship at Joe's Inn, where my communion sacrament is usually three eggs scrambled, sausage patties, home fries, and biscuits, along with Bloody Marys so cheap they must be leaving out the vodka.

Custalow comes along with Cindy and me. R.P. McGonnigal and Cindy's brother, Andy, meet us there. And, as what the TV folks redundantly call an added bonus, Goat Johnson is making a rare appearance. He comes to town maybe three times a year to see his old buds and do some fund-raising for that college up in Ohio that, for no sane reason, has made him its president. It's an Oregon Hill reunion in full force.

R.P. has brought along Tommy, his latest flame. They got there early enough to get the big table in the back. By the time we arrive, Goat is already sucking the air out of the room, telling some shaggy-dog story involving himself and the wife of a multimillionaire alum by whom Goat's college hopes to be remembered posthumously.

"Damn, Goat," Andy says, "you're telling them same friggin' stories you told forty years ago, except now they're starring cougars instead of sophomores."

"Once a bullshitter, always a bullshitter," I offer by way of hello.

"I can't tell you," Andy says, "how much it pains me to see my innocent baby sister doing the Sunday morning walk of shame with a lowlife like Willie Black."

Cindy notes that his extramarital shenanigans pretty much killed the whole concept of shame for the Peroni family, along with Andy's first marriage. Nothing much is sacred on Sunday morning at Joe's when the Bloody Marys start coming hot and heavy.

Pretty soon, talk turns to Dark Star and the recent unpleasantness. Hell, it's Topic A anywhere in town. A couple of guys I hardly know stop by individually to ask me what the "real story" is, like we're holding out on our readers.

Tommy, R.P.'s friend, speaks up. I don't think I've heard him talk up till this point.

"I knew that guy, sort of."

"Biggio?" I ask.

"Yeah. He was, like, a friend of a friend."

We all wait for more. Finally Tommy realizes that his vocal skills are still in demand.

"My friend used to say he had a screw loose," Tommy offers. Urged on, he gives us a for-instance.

"One time, he was supposed to have just up and disappeared. The way I heard it, he took off in his car one day. Didn't anybody, even his wife, know where he went."

After a too-long silence, McGonnigal says, "Well, what happened then?"

"He came back, but they never did find the car."

Tommy's not one to tell more than he has to, but his vignette kind of reinforces the general opinion that the late Mr. Biggio had batshit issues, something I hope to nail down further as soon as we finish embellishing the old, old stories and I drop Cindy and Abe off at the Prestwould.

First, though, I check my cell phone to see if I've missed any calls. Cindy and pretty much everyone I know at the paper keeps after me to get an iPhone, presumably because my life won't be complete until I can receive e-mails on my phone. But I'm happy with my flip-top cell. Sure, the back comes off sometimes, but that's why God made duct tape.

The only call I missed hearing in the din at Joe's is from Sally, who says they have definite and irrefutable confirmation now that the guy in the plane was indeed David Biggio. No surprise there.

"Any chance you might have something for us on his former wife or anyone else who knew him?"

I could tell her I'm on my way to waylay the ex-wife now, but I wouldn't want to get my city editor's hopes up and then dash them. Once I'm sure it's her, we can talk.

"You might want to step it up," she says. "The dragon lady is scorching us pretty good. She's wondering where the hell you are."

She says it low enough that I figure Rita Dominick is terrorizing the newsroom at present.

"On my day off?"

"Well, I'm just saying, she's here and loaded for bear."

"Good reason to stay out of the office."

"Yeah, I should have been so smart. Oh, yeah. What about that guy down in East Bumfuck? The one that had his plane stolen. Snapper?"

"Chopper. Chopper Ware. Chopper from Topping. I'm on that too."

Unlike our publisher, Sally Velez knows that when I say I'm on it, I'm on it. She urges me to get results as soon as possible, before Ms. Dominick fires what is left of the newsroom. Sally's reward for coming into the joint on a Sunday is an ass-chewing by our ultimate boss, who skipped all the grades where you learn how to treat human beings.

In twenty minutes, I'm parked outside the residence of Robert and Louisa Klassen on a middle-class street halfway between the Boulevard and the Downtown Expressway. Normally, it's a ten-minute trip, but the streets near the late Dark Star are either blocked by police barriers or crowded with cars driven by the kind of people who slow down on the interstate to gawk at wrecks.

It's a quarter till one. As good a time as any to barge into someone else's business. Hey, it's what I do.

I'm not sure anyone's home. If I were in the former Ms. Biggio's shoes, I might be taking a long vacation right now. She has to know it's only a matter of time until somebody, either a cop or a reporter, comes knocking.

The man who answers the door after a long minute or so looks a little younger than me and a lot bigger. He has on a cutoff T-shirt and has tattoos on both his shoulders. The one on his left arm is a Confederate battle flag. The one on his right arm says "Fuck With Me." He does not look like a "people person."

"What do you want?" he asks, and I know I'd better do like my tweeting-addicted coworkers and state my case in 140 characters or less.

"I'm a reporter. I know Louisa Klassen was married to David Biggio. Soon, everyone will, including the cops. I just want a few facts."

He tells me to get the hell off his property and leave his wife alone.

I tell him, as quickly as I can before he either slams the door or steps outside to kick my ass, that her name will be in the paper tomorrow, one way or the other. He has to know this was coming, but he looks like he's ready to shoot the messenger. Literally.

Just then, Louisa Klassen appears, kind of pushing her husband aside and filling up the third of the doorway he's not already occupying.

"All I want is to be left alone," she says.

I know from the record she's either thirty-six or thirty-seven. She looks a little older, with some gray roots to her blonde hair and a brow creased by frown wrinkles. She could use some time at a gym maybe she can't afford.

I wish I could leave her alone. I explain that I can't and still keep my job. I tell her that others probably will be beating a path to her door very soon. And that they'll want to know all about her and David Biggio's daughter.

"You leave Brandy out of this," she says. She starts to cry.

Bobby Klassen steps in front of her and backs me down off the front steps. I manage to hand a card to Louisa before I retreat to my aging Honda without the threatened knuckle sandwich. I ask her, looking around her red-faced husband, to please call me so we can talk, before the hordes descend.

"Anybody that comes here has got to go through me," Mr. Klassen says. I feel sorry for them both, putting off the inevitable. Everybody with a muckraking website or off-brand cable "news" show is going to want to hear about the guy who took out twenty-two of his fellow human beings with a twin-engine Beechcraft. And who better to tell them all about him than his loving ex-wife?

And I'll be the guy who blows their cover. If I didn't know somebody else would do it if I didn't, I might just let them hide away. Maybe.

I go back to the office. Sarah's there, and she seems relieved when I tell her that I've found David Biggio's former wife.

"Did you talk to her?"

"Not really. I don't know if she will talk. I gave her my card. Her husband is a little testy."

"So we're going to just tell everybody who she is?"

"Yeah," I say, "who she is, where she lives, who her second husband is, who her kid is, the usual stuff."

"She had a kid with Biggio?"

I nod.

"A daughter."

"But no interview."

Not yet, I tell her. But there was something I saw in Louisa Klassen's eyes that made me think she was not as determined to barricade the door as her husband is.

I've written the story for the Monday paper, with precious little more information than we had this morning. Sarah has managed to dig up details of Biggio's early life—where he went to school, his thwarted attempt to get a degree from one of our fine state universities, some bits and pieces about his working career, broad hints of mental illness.

Baer has a story about the memorial service for all the victims that's scheduled for tomorrow. My only contribution is the news that Biggio's ex-wife lives in the same general area where he crashed that plane two days ago, and that there is a daughter, who would be about twelve now, if Jumpin' Jimmy's memory serves.

My instincts about Louisa Klassen weren't wrong. Just before nine o'clock, as I'm finishing my contribution to tomorrow's stories, my geriatric cell phone goes off.

"Mr. Black?"

It sounds like she's talking low enough to keep someone else from hearing her.

"Ms. Klassen?"

"Louisa. Are you really going to put my name in your paper tomorrow?"

"Yes. I'd like to talk to you, though, before I do that, if I could."

"Bobby's really going to be mad as hell when he finds out I called you."

"But you want to tell me something about David."

"He's not a monster. He's not like they say on the TV. He's not some kind of psychotic killer."

I don't argue the point, although twenty-two victims' next of kin certainly would.

I make a deal I hope I can keep.

"If you can give me an interview tomorrow," I tell her, "we won't run your name until Tuesday. That'd at least give you and your husband time to maybe leave town for a week or two, until this dies down."

"We were thinking about doing that. Bobby's got a sister up in Pennsylvania, and we've both got some leave time coming. And we need to get Brandy out of here for a while."

"But if I keep your name out of my paper tomorrow, you've got to meet with me tomorrow morning."

She's silent for a few seconds, then tells me she will meet me at a coffee shop in Carytown at nine.

"How are you going to square that with your husband?"

"I'll tell him I made a deal."

"If you aren't there, I'll put something up on our website at five after nine."

"If I tell somebody I'll do something, I do it," she says.

Give Rita Dominick credit. She does have a strong work ethic, much to our chagrin. She left for a while in the afternoon, but, like flu season and taxes, she's back.

When I tell her that we can't release Louisa Klassen's name and location for another day, she has a hissy fit. Only after I have assured her that we will have an exclusive from the one person who might have known him better than anyone else does she relent.

"This," she says to me as she leaves, we hope for the final time, "had better be good."

I CALL Cindy to let her know I will be coming home at some point.

"I'll call the FBI and tell them to call off the search."

She says she and Custalow are watching some Netflix movie I'm probably just as happy to miss. There is a lot of dialogue in it, I am told, and nothing blows up. She says it's almost over and that Abe is snoring. I tell her I'll be there soon.

I try Kate's number. She answers herself this time.

There isn't much I can say that doesn't sound like bullshit, but I do feel like I have to make the effort.

"Do you know anything else?" she asks me.

I tell her that we've located his former wife, and that we're still trying to get an interview with the guy over in Topping whose plane crashed into the building. And I mention that there is every indication that David Biggio was not of sound mind.

"So it was just some nut who decided to play kamikaze? That's all it was?"

"I don't know, Kate. We're still trying to find out."

"You know, I wasn't very nice to Greg. I wasn't a good wife. I know that."

She sounds like she's been crying and is about to do some more.

I assure her that she's a good person, that she was a good wife, and is a great mom. I tell her that I know, from firsthand experience, that it's not easy getting along with somebody else twenty-four hours a day.

"Yeah," she says. "Maybe there are people that just shouldn't get married at all. Maybe we're those people."

"We had a lot of good times," I remind her, "and I'm sure you had a lot of good times with Greg."

"I'm trying to keep the good times front and center."

That, I tell her, is an excellent idea.

"One thing, though," she says. "Please try to find out what the hell happened, and why."

That, I assure her, will be my main reason for living for the foreseeable future.

CHAPTER FOUR

Monday

The coffee place on Cary isn't in Starbucks's league, gouging-wise, but it's making an effort. I'm so used to drinking the sludge we mainline at the paper that I can't appreciate good java anyhow, but I'm paying for it nonetheless.

I get here at a quarter till nine, and Louisa Klassen is already inside waiting for me. It's starting out to be a pretty nice day for April, but she says she'd rather stay indoors, like she already thinks people are on the prowl for her. She looks worried. She's wearing sunglasses, and she keeps glancing over her shoulder and surveying the street outside.

So we find a place in the corner. The only person within earshot of us has earbuds, listening to his favorite music while he works on the Great American Novel. I've heard about people squatting in these places, ordering one cup of cappuccino and staying put for four hours. Well, at these prices, maybe they feel entitled.

I buy her a latte and myself the closest thing I can find to actual no-pedigree coffee. I don't care whether it was grown in the shade or not. I even spring for a couple of muffins. Actually the coffee is pretty good, relatively speaking.

Louisa's hands are shaking so badly that she has to use both of them to drink the latte.

"You weren't followed, were you?" I ask.

"No." She looks around again. "Why?"

"Because you look like you're about to jump out of your skin."

She puts the latte down and takes off the sunglasses.

"I shouldn't be talking to you."

I go over the main reasons she should. One, she can give our readers a picture of what her ex-husband was really like, make him into a human being. Whatever she says can't be worse than what people are thinking. Two, it's buying her some time so that she, her daughter, and the lovely Mr. Klassen can get out of town before the news locusts descend on them.

"I feel like Lee Harvey Oswald's wife," she says. "I saw a thing on the History Channel, and she was just sitting there, cringing, like it was all her fault. You knew her life was going to be crap from there on out."

She looks, fixing me with these brilliant blue eyes that almost make up for the wrinkles and bad dye job.

"But he wasn't like that."

"Tell me."

Louisa and David Biggio were married five years. The first couple, she says, were pretty good. He was twenty-nine and she was twenty-one when they tied the knot. Doing the math, I realize she's younger than she looks.

"I was a junior at VCU. He kind of swept me off my feet. He could be charming as hell, and he was good-looking back then. He wanted to get married right away, so I dropped out. I keep meaning to go back, but it's so expensive now."

She's tearing her napkin into tiny little shreds, a pile of confetti that grows on the table in front of her as I try not to look. I relate for her Andi's long, long slog through college.

"Good for her," Louisa says when I tell her that graduation day for my daughter is finally a possibility. "It'll mean a lot to her."

It'll mean a lot to me too, I want to say, like no more tuition bills, but I guide the conversation back to her late ex-husband.

She says that she knew early in their relationship that he'd had some kind of breakdown when he was in college, which was why he never finished either. He was working as a draftsman when she met him.

"His family kind of downplayed his past, uh, issues. And you know what they say, about love being blind and all."

Things started going downhill the Christmas of their third anniversary, she says. He had to take the treatment at Tucker's, the time-honored rest stop for Richmonders with head issues.

After Tucker's, though, "He seemed to be OK again for a while. The medication helped him, but he kind of hated it, and he'd go off it now and then. I tried to keep an eye on him, but you get tired of asking a grown man every morning, 'Did you take your meds today?'

"And then I got pregnant with Brandy."

I ask Louisa about flying. I knew David Biggio didn't just go out to some half-ass airport last Friday and decide he was a pilot.

She says his father owned a plane, and that David had been flying since he was fourteen years old. At some point after the Tucker's sojourn, they did take his pilot's license away, but he still managed to get some buddy to let him fly once in a while.

"He said it was the only time he felt like he was really free. I guess he meant from whatever demons kept slipping back into his head."

I don't mention how unfortunate it was that the demons seemed to come back when he was a mile off the ground piloting more than a ton of airplane.

He was never violent with her, she says, although she did move out of the house on a couple of occasions after the baby was born, just to be on the safe side, when things got bad. He lost a couple of jobs, but he was charming and smart, and he was never unemployed for long.

But the idea of spending the rest of her life dealing with schizophrenia eventually wore her down.

"I filed for divorce in 2005, and it was granted the next year. Brandy was two years old."

I mention that I had heard something about a road trip and a car that disappeared forever.

"How did you know about that?" she asks. I tell her I have big ears.

He came home one day and said he'd been laid off.

"He didn't seem that concerned about it, actually seemed like it was grounds for celebration.

"We got a babysitter and went out for dinner that night, the Robin Inn I think, and he drank a little more than he usually did. He got a little loud, and the waitress came over and asked him to hold it down. He found out the table next to us had complained, and he wound up getting in a fight, I mean an actual fistfight, with these two guys."

Between the time the cops were called and their arrival, David Biggio took a powder. I guess he forgot he had a wife who needed a ride home.

"I walked. It wasn't terribly far, but I was upset. And when I got there, David and the car were gone. The babysitter was scared to death."

He turned up in a Texas jail two months later with no recollection of what might have happened to his ride.

"It was not long after that, after he got back on his meds, I told him I was leaving and taking the baby. I knew it was just going to keep happening over and over."

He fought the divorce, and especially custody arrangements. Things got ugly. Louisa says she hired a lawyer, and the lawyer managed to make the judge aware of some of the more embarrassing facts about his mental illness.

"They were mean to him," Louisa says. "I didn't intend for them to humiliate him like that. I mean, I knew I couldn't live with him, but I still loved him."

The napkin has been completely converted into scraps by this time, and Louisa looks like she's about to cry. I fish my amazingly clean handkerchief out of my pants pocket.

"Thank you," she says.

Other than that one night at the Robin Inn, Louisa Biggio says she never saw her husband act overtly violent toward anyone, although I feel certain that he didn't get thrown in that Texas jail for jaywalking. That only happens to African Americans, apparently.

But he did do a bit of stalking.

"After he accepted the divorce, he was gone somewhere for about six months. Nobody knew exactly where. His mother and father and his brother didn't really want him around anymore. I was afraid he'd pulled another Texas stunt. But then he showed up again one night on my doorstep. Bobby had moved in by then. He said he wanted to see Brandy, but Bobby and I didn't think that was such a good idea."

She got a restraining order, but neither that nor her big new tattooed love interest seemed to keep him away.

Finally she had him arrested. He went on trial for stalking. Instead of accepting some kind of plea bargain, he insisted on taking it to court. He further insisted on being his own lawyer.

"It was awful," Louisa says. "My lawyer brought out all this embarrassing stuff that he'd done, all the way back to when he was a kid, things his family never told me, probably because they were afraid it would have scared me away from marrying him."

He got a six-month sentence and served three of that. He was assured, more than ever, of not seeing his daughter again.

"After that, it seemed like he transferred whatever grudge he had against me to the lawyers. He would write me, maybe every six months or so, and he was always ranting about the 'damn vultures.' I never wrote him back. I was married to Bobby by then. And he finally stopped."

Louisa says she had no idea where her ex-husband was living after that, other than postmarks, which usually were from places out near the Chesapeake.

"I think he moved around a lot. I wish he'd have moved farther away."

She says both his mother and father have died in the ten years between their divorce and now, and that his brother has moved, she believes, to another state.

"They had a little money, and I guess the brother got all of that. I heard that they disowned David."

I asked her last night if she would bring a picture of him from when they were married. I remind her, and she digs into her purse and comes out with a photograph of David Biggio, circa 2003. He was handsome. In the photo we managed to get courtesy of the DMV from two years ago, he looks twenty years older. He's mostly bald, looks a little unfocused, and has more frown wrinkles than his ex-wife. The last few years have been hard on both of them.

"Bobby doesn't know I kept a picture of him," she says. "I'd appreciate it if you didn't tell anybody where you got it. And I want it back."

I can't imagine anyone would think I got it from anyone other than her, but I do promise.

I asked her if she ever thought about her ex-husband after she finally was able to extricate him from her life.

She gives me a sharp look, and her frown wrinkles seem to multiply.

"I probably shouldn't say this," she says, clenching the handkerchief, "and you better not quote me, but I thought about him every day."

When we part, she looks both ways as she exits the coffee shop, then checks the sidewalk before scurrying down the side street to her car.

THE MEMORIAL service is at one. It's supposed to be for all the victims, but the main thrust seems to be to remember the lost legal brain trust from Bartley, Bowman and Bush. There will be other, separate funerals later, but this is the one for show. I see trucks and cars with the insignias of all the local TV stations along with a couple from out of town.

They hold it at the Altria Center, which used to be the Mosque before it was decided that naming an entertainment center after a Muslim place of worship might irritate the eminently irritable followers of Islam. Hell, I still call it the Mosque, more of habit than disrespect. Elvis sang there. Sinatra almost died there.

It's right across Monroe Park from the Prestwould, so I have time to stop by and pick up Cindy. She makes me put on a tie and find a sports jacket that doesn't have noticeable spaghetti-sauce stains.

A handful of other Prestwouldians accompany us. Clara Westbrook, who shouldn't be walking that far, is accompanied by the Barons, my former neighbors. They all knew some of the departed. When twenty-two people get taken out in one rather spectacular swoop, you find out what a small town Richmond really is.

I estimate that there are a couple of thousand people in attendance. Four different ministers talk, and each seems to be trying to top the one before in long-windedness. I look around and see Mark Baer sitting down low. He's actually covering the services. I'm here because, well, it's my damn story. I want to know as much about this whole godforsaken disaster as I can.

On the front row, among the other bereaved family members, I can see the back of Kate's head. Her mother and father are flanking her. They've wisely left three-year-old Grace with a sitter.

When all the preachers have run out of breath and we've sung all the appropriate songs, it's almost three. I am allegedly off today, so I don't think the powers that be will mind too much if I come in a bit late to do the story they're getting for free.

Cindy and I are talking with Fred Baron when I realize Kate, briefly *sans* parents, is standing about ten feet away. I excuse myself and go over to speak. The two BB&B lawyers who are offering their condolences move away.

"Are you OK?" I ask her.

"As good as can be expected."

She sighs and looks around.

"I feel like such a hypocrite," she says. "I mean, we were trying to, quote, work it out and all, but I don't have the right to mourn like those women do."

She nods toward a large cluster encircling the wives of two of the partners.

"I mean, those gals, they were there for the long haul, probably forty years or more. And somehow I couldn't make it through five years with Greg."

Her voice trips on his name. Out of instinct, I put my arm around her. Out of instinct, she lets me for a moment.

Looking over her shoulder, I see Cindy looking our way. It is not a benign look.

After a few seconds, I let go, and her parents come over to whisk her away from the likes of ex-husbands. They don't speak.

Fred Baron has gone back to get the car for Clara, who has bitten off a bit more than she can chew, walking-wise. I escort Cindy back to the Prestwould before going in to write my story.

"What was that about?" she asks me.

I could ask, "What was what all about?" but not without blushing.

"I thought she needed a hug."

"So I see."

I attempt, the best I can in our short walk, to assure Cindy Peroni that she is the only woman in my life other than my mother and daughter.

A smarter man would have left it at that.

"But we were married for three years. You can't just turn it on and off."

Oops.

Cindy raises an eyebrow.

"You probably could," she says, "if you really tried."

Cindy has forgiven me for a multitude of sins in our vine-tangled journey to cohabitation. I am getting the impression that having feelings for one of my three ex-wives would not fall into the category of "forgivable."

I emphasize, perhaps a bit too loudly, that the fact that I feel sorry for Kate does not mean I have any desire whatsoever to crawl back into her bed. Cindy tells me to keep my voice down.

We're both silent for a couple of minutes. Then she takes my hand in hers and tells me she's sorry.

"But I can't help but worry. I mean, she's younger than me, she's a damn lawyer while I'm just trying to get a degree and maybe teach sixth-graders. And she's hot."

"Not as hot as you."

If you talk enough, eventually you say the right thing.

Walking toward the paper and sucking on a Camel, I check my messages and see that Sally Velez has been trying to get in touch with me.

"You rang?" I ask, when I get to the newsroom.

"Don't you ever answer that thing?" She points to the cell phone in my hand.

I explain that it is considered bad form to take phone calls during memorial services.

"Oh, you went? You're not covering it though."

I tell her that I know very well that the capable Mr. Baer was representing our newspaper, and that what I'll be writing is an interview with the former Louisa Biggio.

Sally's face brightens.

"Thank God. Dominick's been on my ass all day about that."

I tell her to consider her ass unburdened.

The story isn't that hard to write. It's bound to sell a few papers. People love to read about people crazier than themselves.

Sarah comes up and asks me if I've had any luck getting in touch with Chopper Ware. After determining who and where he was, she and I have both been unable to raise him by phone, and covering other aspects of the story has kept either of us from taking a road trip to Topping.

She has been in touch with the families of several of the victims, so that we can give them at least a fraction as much attention as we are giving the asshole who killed them. It is a losing battle that honest journalists wage. Everyone says newspapers run too much bad news, that they want more feel-good stories. Every readership survey and all empirical wisdom says the opposite. So we give 'em what they want: Screaming A1 headline on the killer—who he was, what his family is like—and a piece inside the paper two days later with short bios on the people he destroyed.

"One of the young couples," Sarah says, "had a two-year-old. They got a babysitter so they could celebrate their third wedding anniversary. One of the ones that isn't supposed to make it, they haven't told him yet his wife is dead."

We spend some of our most energized days trying to wring a modicum of sense out of something like this, making a detailed accounting of horror and loss.

It is enough to make a weak-willed person turn to drink.

When I make it known that a trip to Topping is in order, Sarah asks if she can come along. I ask her if she likes fried seafood.

I'M BACK home by eight. In cold, dark weather I drive, but today the sun's just setting as I start my ten-block walk. When I get up to our little love nest, there's a glorious sunset exploding out the windows facing Monroe Park.

"Come here, look at this," Cindy says every five minutes or so. I ask her if the view's any different than it was the last time she roused me. And it always is. The colors change before your eyes. It's almost enough to make you believe the world has some redeeming qualities.

I try Chopper Ware's number one last time. I'll drive down there tomorrow anyhow, but it would be good to know I'm not wasting my time.

This time, someone answers.

I ask to speak to James Ware.

"Who the hell wants him?"

The guy has a sandpaper voice that sounds like it might have been strained through a sea of bourbon.

I explain who I am and what I am.

"Damn, you people are like cockroaches. You're everywhere," he says.

He goes on to tell me that I'm the fourth "asshole reporter-type" to call him. He's just gotten back in from a day on the bay fishing, and the phone's been ringing off the hook.

I emphasize that I'm from "his" paper, since our paper is about the only one you can buy in Topping, and that we just wanted to get his side of "this tragedy."

"Tragedy is right!" He booms it so loud I have to hold the phone a foot away from my ear. "Who's gonna pay for my plane?"

If I were to drive down there tomorrow, I ask, fingers crossed, would he be willing to give me a few minutes of his time? I tell him I would hate for some Yankee carpetbagger from Washington or Baltimore or somewhere up north to come down and get everything all wrong.

He hesitates.

Maybe he figures saying yes to one of us will get him off the hook, because he finally says, "OK. I'll give you twenty minutes. You gonna pay me for this?"

I tell him I'll bring him a fifth of Early Times.

He laughs.

"Make it Knob Creek and you got a deal. But I tell you, I can't shed a whole lot of light on this fella. He kind of kept to himself. And it ain't James. Everybody calls me Chopper."

He tells me he's an early riser, and that I might have the best chance of catching him if I get there before nine. I thank Chopper for agreeing to talk to me, hopefully before he tells his story to a whole pack of out-of-state competitors. Our publisher definitely would not like to read Chopper Ware's take on his late tenant in the *Washington Post.*

Neither would I.

Mr. Ware might not know a hell of a lot about David Biggio. However, considering how little anyone else seems to know about where he's been the last nine years or so, he's the best option I have right now.

I call Sarah Goodnight and tell her to set her alarm clock for six tomorrow.

CHAPTER FIVE

Tuesday

I check my e-mail by the dawn's early light and get the sad news that two more of Friday's victims have died overnight, including the poor sap who never knew his wife predeceased him. So we have an even two dozen now.

There are plenty of murders around here, one or two a week year-round, but most of them come with a reasonable explanation. Usually, a drug deal or an intimate relationship went bad. But when twenty-four people doing nothing worse than celebrating Friday get burned up by someone who, to my knowledge, none of them knew, it makes for the kind of story you can't take your eyes off, no matter how heartbreaking and grisly it is.

It might just be a catastrophically stupid accident. The guy knew how to fly, but he might not have been in the cockpit much lately. Or he could have just decided to end it all and take a few strangers with him. My thought, though, is that he had something in mind, or he wouldn't have stolen Chopper Ware's plane. And there's the fact that his ex-wife and his daughter lived close enough by to feel the heat from Daddy's little massacre.

I'm pondering this as I drive to Sarah's apartment. The Camel I'm sucking on helps kick-start my brain. At least that's what I tell myself when I try to self-justify my habit.

Sarah's place is just a few blocks west of Boulevard off Monument, not that far from the scene of our city's latest unpleasantness. She'd been to Dark Star a few times herself.

Her building offers much more in location than it does in ambience. It's the kind of place where the landlord says, if you want to paint it, he'll pay for the paint. I haven't been inside it for some time. I have enough bad habits and, frankly, my charm stock is ebbing while hers is rising. It's easier to be good when temptation gives you a wide berth. As we both grow a little older, she's up to more than half my age now.

She must have been watching from one of the windows, because she's outside before I can cut the engine off. When I open the door, I can still smell the smoke from four days ago.

Another kind of smoke has Sarah's attention though.

"Jesus, Willie," she says, sniffing the nicotine air as she leans in. "You're never going to be able to sell this thing. Are you even throwing the butts out, or do you have them all saved in the backseat?"

I ask her if she'd rather bitch or ride.

"OK," she says, plopping her pretty butt into the passenger's seat, "but you're going to cost me a trip to the dry cleaner's."

She already knows about the other two Dark Star deaths too. She even found time to post something about it to our website.

"So what do you think?" she asks. "I mean, what happened?"

It could have been an accident, I offer, but it isn't my present opinion.

"One thing," I tell her, "is the sheer fucking bad luck of it. You read about people crashing private planes into neighborhoods. It happens. But who does a bull's-eye on a packed bar at happy hour?"

"Well, I'd say it definitely was a suicide," she says. "The only question is whether it was something else."

The cops aren't telling us much, as usual. I imagine they're just now learning that his ex-wife lived in the neighborhood, along with some of the finer details of how he lost his family and, apparently, his mind. If I weren't headed east into the early morning sun, L.D. Jones and I might be having a chat about now. Nothing makes the chief less happy than learning about a case's latest developments in his daily newspaper. Cornflakes probably have been spit out and bad words uttered at the Jones residence.

I express the hope that Bobby and Louisa Klassen are already at that house in Pennsylvania, away from the prying eyes of nosy-ass reporters and neighbors for a while at least.

Sarah shifts and turns toward me.

"So he knew where his ex-wife lived. Maybe he was aiming for her place?"

"It's possible," I allow. "Maybe he went in low and then just lost control. But he hadn't been seen by the wife in years."

"He must have been pretty pissed about losing any rights to see his daughter."

"Yeah. Louisa said he really threw a fit in court. Didn't help his chances of future visits any. But he seemed like he'd given up on that front. He just kind of disappeared."

We head east on I-64, down into the swampland. The traffic isn't so bad today, once we get out of the city. In a month or so, the vacationers headed to Virginia Beach or the Outer Banks will make this a parking lot, but today you can actually enjoy the scenery.

We pass Colonial Downs, which used to be a racetrack, before the horse owners and the guys running the place had a disagreement over how many actual races they should run a year. Too bad. It was a great place to sit with friends, make a bet every half hour or so, and, if you were so inclined, step outside and smell the horse doody.

We turn off onto Route 33 and soon are approaching West Point, which is as beautiful a spot as you'll find in eastern Virginia. The York River splits into the Pamunkey and the Mattaponi here. From the bridges, you can see wetlands in all directions. But you need to breathe through your mouth.

I had neglected to warn Sarah.

"Good God," Sarah says. "Who died?"

I explain about the paper mill that fuels the town's economy.

"They say it smells like money," I offer.

"It smells like something. Maybe you ought to fire up another Camel, to cover the stink."

I tell her a joke you should only tell someone of the opposite sex if you've shared the sheets with her.

"A Virginia Tech guy takes his date out parking. They're going at it hot and heavy, and she says, 'Oh, Baby. Kiss me where it smells bad.' So he drives her to West Point."

Ba-da-bum.

She pretends to be offended, but then I see her mouth twitch, and I hear a snort.

"Oh," she says, "that was pretty funny. Gross and tacky, but funny."

If you're going to be gross and tacky, I tell her, funny doesn't hurt.

Soon we're past our olfactory bump in the road, going through Glenns and Saluda, passing the turnoff for Urbanna, where the oyster festival every October is almost worth the traffic jam that leads to it.

By a little past eight, we turn off on Route 3, and I start looking for the road leading to Chopper Ware's place. I got his address and some half-ass directions and did a Google map of it. (No, I explain to Sarah, for the second time, I don't have GPS. Shoot me.)

We pass it twice before I find the right road. We follow it through the woods and come out the other side on a little hill that overlooks the mouth of the Rappahannock. The view exceeds the one in West Point, and it doesn't smell bad.

The house sits at the high point of the hill, surrounded by a picket fence. It has two chimneys and a big, wide porch offering the much-coveted water views in three directions. Down below us, in the distance, are more modest cottages and what appears to be a dock.

It's almost eight thirty by the time we park in the big circular driveway. I'm hoping Chopper Ware didn't decide to go to work a little early this morning.

I hear Chopper before I see him.

"Well," I hear him bellow, making Sarah jump, "I see you finally got here. Thought maybe you got lost. You city folks can't find your ass with both hands."

Chopper Ware looks like a guy who just wandered out of the woods after a very long absence. The beat-up Panama hat he's wearing and the flowing white beard hide most of his sun-baked face. Sunglasses cover the majority of what the hat and whiskers don't. He's the kind of guy that you can't tell how old he is, kind of a Leon Russell look. And he looks like he's about eighty pounds overweight. Trying to read something from what we can see, I reach the conclusion that Mr. Ware is a man who hoards his smiles.

I hand him the promised fifth of Knob Creek. That fifth didn't come cheap. I had to rely on Bootie Carmichael, our old-fart sports columnist and drinker extraordinaire. By the time I realized last night that I wouldn't be able to hit an open ABC store before we got here this morning, I figured, correctly, that Bootie might be a person who would have a full bottle of Knob Creek lying around. Bootie is inordinately afraid of running out of liquor. He made me pay him ten bucks more than it cost him.

"Don't worry, Hoss," Bootie said as I was leaving his house. "You can turn in an expense form for it."

I remind Bootie, who probably got the Knob Creek in the first place in exchange for toadying up to one sports team or another, that the company is a little more gimlet-eyed about expenses these days, if he hasn't noticed.

"Well," he said, "you oughta give it a try."

Chopper seems impressed that I've actually come through on my promise. He seems to have low expectations of journalists.

"Come on up," he says, "but you gotta make it quick. I'm due somewhere at nine fifteen."

I realize I haven't introduced my associate.

"This is Sarah Goodnight," I tell him.

"Yes, indeed," he says. He seems to be smacking his lips. "You're the gal that called me."

"Yes, sir."

Chopper waves his hands.

"Don't call me 'sir.' Makes me feel old as shit. I still got some gas in the tank."

He doesn't ask us in. Instead we sit on the front porch, which has the kind of view journalists only get to enjoy as guests.

"This place has been here since 1796," he says. "I bought it when the last family member that gave a shit about it died. Some second cousin or something sold it. I'm trying to fix it up."

He has a ways to go, I want to tell him, but you can see the potential in the old two-story faded beauty with that view of the Chesapeake Bay.

We shoot the shit for a couple of minutes before Sarah asks him about David Biggio.

He points to a one-story wooden cottage that sits about 100 yards down the hill, off to one side.

"He'd been there since, I think, 2010. Naw, it was 2009. Fall of 2009. I know because he was here for all the snow we had that winter. Like to of froze, he said."

Biggio just kind of showed up, Chopper says. He had put an ad in the paper when he realized he could take in a little money by renting it out. Biggio was the first one to respond.

"He was honest with me, as far as he went. He told me he'd had some problems, although I didn't know the full extent until all that mess in Richmond. He paid his rent on time."

Ware shakes his head.

"He was the only one down here that called me Jimmy instead of Chopper."

I ask if we can look around the cottage. He might not have let us anyhow, but he explains that the cops, federal, state, and local, have been all over the last place David Biggio slept, and that it is now a crime scene. When I look closer, I can just make out the yellow tape.

"Did they find anything?" I ask.

"What do you mean? Oh, like a diary with his plans to do a kamikaze with my plane? Not that they've told me."

He says the cops had been all over him too, asking him a million questions he didn't have any answers to.

"Those big-city reporters, they've been bugging the shit out of me too," he says. "But you're the first ones I've let on the porch."

I thank him for that.

He says he didn't have many dealings with Biggio, who had gotten employment at a convenience store in Kilmarnock and sometimes worked on the boats out in the bay. He said he was getting some kind of disability money too.

"He didn't seem like a fella that would do the sort of thing he did. But he was peculiar."

"Peculiar?" Sarah asks.

He turns in her direction.

"Yeah. Peculiar. Like he didn't want anybody much to know anything about who he was or where he came from, although some were able to piece some of it together, something about him losing his wife and little girl. And because I know the pharmacist here and nobody can keep a secret around this damn place, I know he was taking some pretty heavy shit, to keep the devil away, I guess. Maybe he ran out of pills."

Chopper laughs, for the first time in our presence.

"I'd see that light on down there night after night. I don't think he slept much."

We do walk around and peer into the cottage windows, but there's not much to see. Sarah takes some pictures on her iPhone. She even gets Chopper to reluctantly pose for one in front of his house.

I ask our host how his renter was able to steal his plane.

"Oh, hell," he says, "I never lock the place up. And he had been up here a few times, to pay the rent and such. And I guess we talked about the plane. Yeah, I know we did, because he mentioned that he used to fly too.

"But I never imagined in a million years that he'd do what he did. Didn't even think he'd be able to fly a plane anymore. Said he hadn't flown one in like twenty years."

Chopper, who hadn't shown any sentiment to speak of when the subject was David Biggio, seems nearly on the verge of tears when he talks about his lost plane.

"I'd had that baby for thirteen years," he says. "She was my family."

Along those lines, I ask him how long he's been out here, and where he came from. I know he doesn't sound local.

He says he bought the hardware store across the bridge sixteen years ago, around the same time he bought the house.

I ask him if he won the lottery.

He gives me a look and tells me people out here don't ask a lot of nosy questions.

I tell him that's what reporters do.

"No wonder everybody hates your asses," he says.

I remark that he doesn't sound like he grew up around here.

He looks at his watch and tells me that he's got to be somewhere in ten minutes, and that it's a nine-minute drive.

Sarah thanks him for his time. He tells her she's too pretty and too nice to be a "goddamn reporter." He looks at me when he says it.

She thanks him for the compliment.

Chopper follows us out to the road in one of those pickups on steroids that are so big they blot out the sun. I wave as we turn in opposite directions. He doesn't seem to reciprocate.

"Well," Sarah says as we head down the road with the sun behind us, "that went well."

We don't talk much about Biggio or Chopper Ware for a bit. I remember that one of my favorite seafood places is just across the Rappahannock bridge. It has a water view and is a hell of a lot closer than Lowry's in Tappahannock.

We're getting ready to tuck into an early lunch of fried everything when Sarah says, "That guy doesn't seem to know much about his tenant."

Maybe, I suggest, he knows more than he's letting on.

"Any reason to think that, other than a terminally suspicious mind?" Sarah asks as she stuffs a hush puppy into her mouth.

Not really, I tell her. It's just that I'm trying to wrap my brain around the fact that this guy Biggio spent the last seven years out here, quiet as a mouse despite his demonstrably bat-shit history, and then suddenly starts hearing voices again, this time telling him he needs to turn a Richmond drinking spot into a human barbecue.

"So what's that got to do with Chopper Ware?"

"I have trouble believing these two guys, both of them living alone next door to each other, one renting from the other, didn't have some kind of personal interaction."

"Maybe he's afraid he'll be implicated. You know, if he had some kind of prior knowledge that the guy was planning to kill a couple of dozen people, he might figure he'd be better off not telling anybody about it later."

"You're probably right," I say as the fried seafood platter is plopped down in front of me, daring me to eat the whole thing. "Sometimes the best answer is the simplest one: David Biggio had been crazy his whole life, and this was what some-body that crazy does sometimes. And if Chopper Ware had known his tenant was planning to fly an aircraft into an occu-pied building, he'd sure as hell have been more careful about keeping him away from the key to his plane."

"Case closed," Sarah says as she fully immerses a shrimp in tartar sauce and dispatches it in one bite.

I tell her she's going to lose her girlish figure if she keeps eating like that.

"Physician," she says, reaching for the sweet iced tea, "heal thyself."

We're back at the paper by two, a good hour before they start paying me to do night cops.

I check in with Sally Velez and tell her I'll have some more insight on Mr. Biggio for tomorrow's readers. She seems pleased.

She tells me Wheelie's been lurking around, asking about every thirty minutes if we have anything else to report.

"I'm sure he's having his ass roasted by lovely Rita," she says, referencing our publisher. "He's just passing it along. Shit flows downhill."

Baer has made some small headway. He's managed to find a couple of people who knew Biggio back in the day, but there's not much they can say about him that his former wife hasn't said already.

"He doesn't seem to have any blood kin around here, or anywhere else, at least none that we've been able to find."

I start to walk away when she stops me.

"Oh, yeah. Chief Jones called. He'd like to talk to you."

I'm sure he would. I turn my cell phone back on and find a couple of missed calls from him on there too.

I take care of some e-mail and have a smoke in the cancer zone outside before giving L.D. a call back. His secretary—excuse me, administrative assistant—says he's busy and can I call him back in ten minutes. I tell her that the chief has my number.

He responds in less than five minutes.

"Busy day?" I ask.

"What the hell are you doing tromping all over my case?"

"Well, L.D., I gave you three days to find the man's ex-wife. What the hell am I supposed to do? Our readers can't wait forever."

"We wanted to talk to her," he says, "and now she's skipped town. And I know damn well you know where she is."

I remind him that it isn't exactly "skipping town" if a person not suspected of any crime takes a little vacation. I further remind him that he and his minions had no clue where Louisa Klassen was until they read about it in the newspaper.

I also tell him that, if I did know where she was, I'd be honor bound not to tell him.

The chief lets me know, rather loudly, that he's got a good mind to have me hauled in and forced to tell what I know under oath. He also says he'd appreciate it if I would keep my ass out of police business. I remind him that police business is sometimes newspaper business too. I further remind him that I always protect my sources. This does not seem to mollify him.

"Show me a little love once in a while, L.D.," I tell him, "and I might be more willing to share."

The chief grunts and hangs up. He knows the rules, and he knows I play by them. He just needs to vent sometimes, especially when it appears that somebody else is doing his job for him.

So Sarah writes about the two deaths, Baer gives the readers a little more insight into Biggio's troubled past, and I give them what I can about the last seven years of a sad and—apparently—lonely life.

Wheelie comes by and congratulates me on finding Ms. Klassen and getting an interview with Chopper Ware.

He says that he guesses we'll be more or less winding this story down, focusing on funerals and weigh-ins from experts on how this sort of thing can happen. They'll all say we need better mental health care. The readers will nod their heads, and the politicians will pay lip service. Then they'll bulldoze Dark Star and put some other joint up in its place. And come time to spend tax money on the aforementioned care, the folks and the pols who depend on their votes will decide they don't need to do anything hasty about mental health care after all.

I tell Wheelie that I still want to check on a couple of things. He groans. While Wheelie knows that I have a pretty good track record when it comes to wrestling the truth to the ground, he knows that he'll probably be the recipient of a Willie-induced headache or two before it's all over. His job would be easier if I'd let this one go and just get back to covering the less spectacular murders that are the subject of most of my stories.

We seem to have a good bead on how our city's worst day in recent history happened. Crazy guy gets crazier when his wife leaves him and takes his only child. He steals a plane and makes some kind of cataclysmic statement a few blocks from where his former family lives.

It seems simple. Sometimes simple is the way to go.

And sometimes it isn't.

CHAPTER SIX

Wednesday

I've been scooped.

I came home shortly after midnight, forgoing Penny Lane or any of my other haunts, choosing instead to climb into bed and cozy up to the warm and lovely body of Cindy Peroni. All seemed right with the world. We would have the interview with Chopper Ware, giving our readers a little more insight into what made the late David Biggio tick. We owned the story.

The phone woke me at six A.M. As soon as I determined that the call was from Wheelie, and that its purpose wasn't to tell me something horrible had happened to Peggy, Andi, or anyone else I care about, I asked him, rather loudly, what the fuck he was doing ringing me up before sunrise and scaring the shit out of me.

That's when he told me about the life-insurance policy.

"I wouldn't have called you," he said, "if lovely Rita hadn't called me already and ordered me to."

It was a blow to us when we lost our last publisher, James H. Grubbs, to what is now referred to as "the Segway incident." We were all sad when Grubby met his untimely end under the wheels of the Number 11 bus. We thought, though, that we might be getting a better deal, publisher-wise. Grubby, who seemed to sell his soul to the corporate devils the minute he left the newsroom for Suitville, could be a pain in the ass.

Our asses didn't know what pain was, though, until Rita Dominick arrived. She's only doing this until our recession-ravaged chain can sell us down the river to some other chain, one that didn't go into hock buying TV stations right before the market crashed. We wonder why she cares so much about the actual journalism we commit, since her main objective is obviously to reduce costs, i.e. staff.

She cares, Sally Velez correctly notes, but not enough to make sure we have adequate staff to do big-boy newspapering.

The life-insurance policy, the reason I just lost a couple of good hours of sleep, plus maybe a little wake-up sex, was paid for by David Biggio. The beneficiary is Brandy Devine Biggio. Our late pilot's twelve-year-old daughter is half a million dollars richer, or will be soon, unless the insurance company can prove that Biggio flew that plane into Dark Star on purpose.

The reason I'm awake now, in the kitchen coaxing a cup of mediocre java out of the coffee-for-dummies Keurig, is that this story is in today's *Washington Post.*

The *Post* has a minuscule presence in Richmond. It is, therefore, somewhat embarrassing when their reporters break any Richmond story before we do. We have the usual reaction when the big-city guys come down here and tromp on our beat. Somehow the one reporter they have working the Dark Star follow-up full time was able to get this information before we—meaning I—did. I do not need Rita Dominick or her proxy interrupting my sleep to make me feel like shit about this turn of events. I do not get beat by the goddamn *Washington Post.* But somehow I did.

They didn't put it on their website until after midnight, and nobody noticed it—or at least nobody in the newsroom did—until the *Post* came out this morning.

Rita Dominick, though, must have checked the *Post* website before she crawled back into her coffin at dawn. She gave Wheelie the WTF call, and he passed it along to me.

Here's the thing though. There isn't a damn thing I can do at six A.M. about getting beat by the *Post*. The only purpose in calling a reporter at this ungodly hour, five hours after his head hit the pillow, is punishment. Rita Dominick and I need to have a discussion, after I've calmed down enough that said conversation won't end in my termination.

There is human tendency to brood over a screwup and make a bad situation worse. I have, I would like to think, evolved beyond that. Getting beat on a story will fry my butt for about the amount of time it takes me to finish this cup of coffee. Then I'll move on.

Bootie Carmichael told me a story one time, after he'd gotten the final score wrong in a Virginia-Virginia Tech basketball game story and nobody caught it on the desk.

He was covering a Washington Redskins game a few years earlier. The Redskins lost when their normally dependable field-goal kicker missed one from almost point-blank range on the last play of the game.

In the postgame interview, somebody had the nerve to ask him if it bothered him.

"The guy just looked at this asshole like he was crazy," Bootie said. "And then he told him, 'Hoss, when it leaves my foot, it leaves my mind.' "

The next week, he kicked a fifty-yard field goal in overtime to put the Skins in the playoffs.

And so, having bounced one off the goalpost, I'm ready to put the next kick right down the middle. Somehow.

Questions abound as I finish that palliative first cup of coffee. How long had Biggio had the policy? Did Louisa Klassen know about it? If so, she sure as hell didn't mention it to me. And how did David Biggio, who did not seem to have much more money than it took to eat and put a roof over his head, come up with the money to pay the premiums?

I read the *Post* article online. The only one of my questions that it answered was the one about when he bought the policy. He purchased it just two weeks before he crashed the plane.

I have a cell phone number for Louise Klassen, wherever she is right now. I intend to have the answer to one of the remaining questions if not both by the time I post tomorrow morning's story.

Cindy comes in and asks me for the gory details. I apologize for waking her up yelling at Wheelie. She shrugs and says she was asleep again five minutes later. I tell her I envy her ability to prioritize.

"Can't let the bastards get you down," she says.

One of Cindy's good qualities, of which there are many, is her ability to shrug off bad tidings and leave past issues where they belong, in the past. The vehicle that Cindy Peroni steers through life does not have a rearview mirror.

Knowing about this, I am sure that, if I am somehow thrown into outer darkness by Cindy, she will not waste much if any valuable slumber time thinking about what might have been. She hardly ever mentions her former husband.

Cindy has had many reasons to hand me my walking papers. If I ever commit an unforgivable sin and find myself outside of that door that says "No reentry," she will not suffer from insomnia.

This makes what I feel I need to do this morning before heading for the paper a bit on the risky side.

Kate and the late Mr. Ellis bought a big-ass place in the West End last year, a few months before they decided to give separation (albeit in the same super-sized house) a try.

Maybe I shouldn't go by. There isn't much I can do to ease her pain, and Cindy would certainly not see this as an act of altruism, which I assure myself it is. You don't live with someone and not feel something, even after it all goes to hell. I see it as sympathy, giving myself, as usual, the benefit of the doubt.

Plus, I really would like to know what made David Biggio crash that particular plane at that particular place at that particular time. I am not a big believer in coincidence. It is possible that Kate can help me on this.

I try Louisa Klassen's cell number and leave a message. I drive by her house. It appears that she and her family are still out of town. I wonder if she knows her daughter probably is about to be $500,000 richer.

There is only one car in the driveway when I get to Kate's. She apparently has sent her parents packing.

She answers the door in a bathrobe, although it's past eleven. I've never seen Kate in anything less than business attire this late on a workday.

She seems a little unfocused. Again, very un-Kate-like.

"Oh, Willie," she says, as if it takes her a few seconds to recognize me. She turns and leads me into the house.

Her daughter is watching television. The house looks as if it has been hit by a small tornado. I wonder to myself why her parents didn't do a little tidying up, since it seems Kate's not quite up to the task.

I ask her how she's doing, as if I don't know.

"Oh, you know," she says, waving her right arm as if all the evidence I need to answer that question is in plain view.

I lead Kate over to the couch and sit in a chair. Grace comes over and sits beside her mother.

"Daddy died," the little girl says, in the same tone she might have used to tell me she's three years old or she's going to the zoo tomorrow. She puts her thumb in her mouth. Kate doesn't stop her, which I'm sure she usually does.

I gradually extract longer and longer answers out of my ex-wife, coaxing her in off the ledge. I find a couple of almost-clean cups and fix us both some coffee. I get a juice box for Grace. When I hug the little girl, she hugs back, hard, like she hasn't gotten much attention lately. Kate always had a tendency to depend on pharmaceuticals when life got to be a bit too much. I thought I'd converted her to the belief that alcohol works better and more dependably, but I fear she's relapsed.

Finally I think the fog has cleared enough to ask her a question that actually requires some thought.

"Was there any reason somebody would have been targeting a bunch of lawyers from BB&B?"

She looks at me like I'm the one who's crazy, but then she sets the coffee cup down.

"I don't know. I mean, lawyers are at the top of everybody's hit list, right next to journalists, no offense. But I hadn't heard anything. You've got to understand, I'm kind of out of the loop. I mean, I have drinks with some of them, but they don't confide much in me—didn't confide much in me—anymore. And Greg never talked much inside baseball with me."

Kate left to pursue what some would call a more righteous form of law. Marcus Green handles the kind of criminal cases that make you look like a genius if you win and an asshole if you don't. Occasionally she and Marcus have effected something close to justice. Sometimes I have helped.

I ask her if Marcus has been around.

"Oh, yeah. He comes by every day. Says I can take all the time I want. I hope he means it."

I ask if the guy who took out her husband and his associates had some reason to hold a grudge against lawyers.

"Well," she says, "I don't think it's possible that Bartley, Bowman and Bush would have been handling a child-custody case. To my knowledge, they've never done anything like that."

She says, though, that she will ask around.

Maybe Biggio just didn't like lawyers. Maybe he was aiming for his former wife's house, although the fact that he somehow found the money to pay the premiums for a half-million-dollar insurance policy in his daughter's name makes that unlikely. He's not going to kill his little girl at the same time he's seemingly trying to make her financially secure.

"Maybe," Kate says, "he was just a crazy son of a bitch who wanted to make everybody else as miserable as he was."

That's still at the top of almost everyone's why'd-he-do-it list. Still I don't know. The Willie radar is tingling. I've learned to listen to it.

We have as normal a conversation as you can have in the aftermath of the obscenely abnormal. Then Kate looks at her watch and says she has to be somewhere. She yawns, and I'm guessing the somewhere is back to bed.

She seems happy enough for me to see my way out. Grace looks at me like she wishes she could go with me.

As Kate stands in the doorway, eager to crawl back under the covers, I stick my big nose a little deeper into my ex-wife's business.

"You're stronger than this."

I stick my foot inside to keep her from closing the door all the way.

Then she does something I have seen her do rarely over the years. She cries. And I don't mean "cries" as in sniffles a little. She's bawling, a regular Niagara Falls. This gets little Grace to bawling too. I step back inside and shut the door.

When she catches her breath, she looks up at me—by this time, I'm trying to hug her and Grace both—and tells me again that she and her now-late husband were unfinished business.

"We were getting back together," she says. "We were working it out. We would have worked it out."

She tells me that Greg spent the night with her just two days before he was killed.

"I told him we needed to go slow, decide if we were both really committed. So he went back to the guest bedroom. If I'd just done what I knew I should have done and told him to stay with me, there's no way he would have gone out drinking Friday afternoon."

I say all of what I hope are the right things. You couldn't have known. You were smart to take it slow. He might have gone to happy hour anyhow and taken you along. Then where would you be? Where would Grace be?

All this might or might not do any good. Grief counselor is not part of my tool kit. But I do make her swear to stay in touch with me and maybe cut back a little on the self-medication.

I kiss her on the forehead, give Grace a kiss on the cheek, and promise to stop by soon.

The newsroom is easing into the day when I get there.

I stop by and ask Wheelie if he'd like to accompany me up to Rita Dominick's office. I've given the publisher's predawn stunt a few hours to get unstuck from my craw, but it's still there. I continue to be royally pissed.

Wheelie grimaces. He's tucking into a late lunch, a meatball sub from the place across the street. I'm afraid it and I are combining to give him a Zantac afternoon.

"You aren't going to do something stupid, are you?" he asks.

"That depends on what you call stupid. Would telling her to have the guts to call me herself the next time she wants to interrupt my sleep be stupid? Would it be stupid to take that one step farther and tell her only an asshole would do something like what she pulled this morning? With your help, I might add."

I have raised my voice a bit, apparently. People are staring. Wheelie tells me to shut the door.

"Don't call her an asshole. Please don't call her an asshole."

"Hey, I'm pulling my punches. Nothing sexist about 'asshole.' It's a nice, pansexual term. Anybody can be an asshole."

He asks me to let him talk to her instead.

"How's that going to work out? You could have told her this morning to cool her jets. You didn't."

Wheelie slams his little plastic fork into his desktop, breaking two of the tines. He looks as sleep-deprived as I feel.

"Hey," he says, "I was half asleep. Give me a break. She is our boss."

Finally he talks me out of throttling our publisher and qualifying for unemployment, but only after he promises me that he will have a serious talk with her about anger management.

"Tell her," I say on my way out, "that I will beat that punk-ass *Post* reporter nineteen times out of twenty, and I don't want to hear any shit from her when I don't bat a thousand."

Wheelie says he will convey that message, although a bit more civilly.

"Maybe," he suggests, "you could use some anger management yourself."

What I need, I tell him, is a good night's sleep and a publisher who doesn't think she's Donald fucking Trump.

I find out how the *Post* got the story on the insurance policy. By pure damn luck, an agent for the company that carried Biggio's policy was blabbing about it at a party, within earshot of somebody who had once met the *Post* reporter and probably wanted to impress him.

The big talker said one of their agents at "some one-horse agency" down near the bay sold Biggio the policy. The guy with big ears told the *Post* guy, who called the agency and got confirmation.

With all the connections I have in this town, this one got past me. So shoot me.

I'm never sure whether Wheelie really had the stones to have that talk with Rita Dominick, but she doesn't come near me for the rest of the evening, which is blessedly quiet.

About ten, I get the call back I was waiting for. Louisa Klassen again sounds as if she is trying not to be overheard.

"Where are you?" I ask.

"We're where I told you we were going. You know, the place up north?"

I want to assure her that her phone is not being tapped.

"I have to make it quick," she says. "Bobby went out for some cigarettes. He says he can't believe how much they cost up here."

Yeah, anybody going north from our tobacco-hugging state should take a few cases along. You could rent a hotel room up there reselling them.

She says to call her back tomorrow, around ten. Her husband's supposed to go out and play golf with his brother-in-law at nine.

I start to tell her about the insurance policy, but she says she hears Bobby's car pulling into the driveway.

There's nothing left to do but rewrite the *Post* story. The only thing I can add that's worth a shit is the fact that Louisa Klassen is at an undisclosed location out of state.

At least nobody else in the fourth estate has found her yet. With little Brandy in line for a half million in insurance money, I'm sure I'm not the only one trying to get some more information from those quarters.

I send my story. About midnight, Sally Velez sees me starting to do a facedown on my keyboard. She tells me to get the hell out of there. If there are any triple homicides, she promises to call me.

"You'll get 'em tomorrow," she says.

I tell her that is my intention.

CHAPTER SEVEN

Thursday

When I call at ten, Louisa Klassen answers on the third ring.

I tell her about the half-million-dollar insurance policy that's coming to her daughter, assuming they can't prove Biggio committed suicide.

She has the kind of reaction you see when those idiots on TV open the door and find the Publishers Clearing House Sweepstakes guy standing there with the big-ass check. Obviously, she doesn't read the *Post* or our rag online.

"Half a million dollars? Are you kidding me? Oh, my God."

She swears she had no idea that her ex-husband had taken out a policy in Brandy's name.

"I mean, why would he? He hadn't seen her in years. This is just too crazy."

I suggest that she and the rest of her family might want to get back to Richmond sometime soon, if for no other reason than to claim their windfall.

"But if they decide it's suicide, then she won't get it?"

More like mass murder with a suicide thrown in, I'm thinking.

"Yeah," I tell her. "I imagine the insurance company is not going to write the check for this one without doing a little investigating."

"David wasn't in his right mind," Louisa says, "but he'd never do what he did on purpose. It had to have been an accident."

I tell her that the cops are still trying to figure that one out but that, for right now, she and her husband won't have to worry about saving for Brandy's college education.

"Bobby's going to flip out when he hears this," she says. I'm thinking her present husband will find a way to spend all that money before his stepdaughter gets out of high school. I can only hope that Louisa will be able to keep his hands off most of it.

I ask her if she can tell me who might have been friends with David Biggio, back when they were married, and especially anybody who might have seen him in the recent past.

She says he didn't have many friends, and most of the ones he had apparently hadn't seen him in years.

"There was one guy," she says, after thinking about it awhile. "I ran into him at Martin's grocery shopping. I think it was last month. Him and his wife used to be close with us, but that kind of went by the wayside after we split up."

The guy, Arthur Heutz, worked with Biggio back in the day. He told Louisa he had run into her ex a couple of months earlier, right before Christmas, when Heutz and his wife were antique hunting out on the Northern Neck.

"They talked a little. He didn't tell me everything he said, but he did tell me that David seemed like he wanted to be somewhere else, like he didn't want anything to remind him of the past.

"I was kind of shocked. I didn't know where David was until Arthur Heutz told me."

I get Heutz's address from her and ask if I can come by when they get back to Richmond.

"I'm not so sure Bobby's going to like that," she says, so I guess I'll just have to charm my way in. I'm so good at that.

"Do you think the police are going to want to talk to me?" she asks.

I assure her that the police, a bunch of nosy reporters, and probably an insurance investigator or two will be stopping by.

She sighs.

"I guess we might as well head back and face the music then."

Louisa Klassen, who has done nothing worse that marry the wrong man at least once, is probably in for a rough patch, privacy-wise. Blustering Bobby probably will miss my good manners and social skills by the time he, his wife, and step-daughter get through dealing with what awaits them.

I CALLED Louisa on the landline. Because I didn't use my cell phone, shit happens.

I'm walking out of the study when Cindy meets me at the door.

"What the hell is this?" she asks, not very pleasantly.

I tell her it's my cell phone, which she is holding in her hand. Then I look at it more closely. Oh.

Apparently Kate took me up on my offer to help, or at least lend a sympathetic ear. She texted me.

"Thanks for coming by. It meant a lot. Call me."

Cindy was not aware that I had visited my ex-wife yesterday until she heard the "ping" and looked at my cell, lying there on the coffee table for all to see.

I try doing the hummina-hummina, but there isn't much I can say that will negate what's right there, staring me in the face on my own phone.

"Look," I say, when she stops yelling so she can catch her breath, "I'm going to have to work with Kate on this. She knows all those lawyers at BB&B, the ones who died and the ones still there, and if anybody can figure out why all this happened, it's her."

"And you're the only goddamn reporter who can interview her."

"Well I'm the one who knows her the best."

"Intimately, you might say."

"Well, we were married."

Maybe it wasn't the best strategy to state the obvious. I try again to assure Cindy that intimacy with my ex is a thing of the long-buried past, not mentioning our one-time rekindling a couple of years ago. That exclusion, I thought, was smart of me.

We go round and round on it. Cindy has her back up, and maybe I do too.

"Maybe I ought to go back to my place for a while," she says. "That way, if you want to bring your ex over for some up-close-and-personal, I won't be in the way."

I tell her she's being ridiculous. I tell her that her unwarranted suspicions are why I didn't tell her about talking with Kate in the first place.

Cindy probably could be appeased by a better, more patient Willie. But I have my mind too much on the whole Biggio mess. I need to find Arthur Heutz, and I need to try to find out more about that insurance policy. I need to do both those things and put in eight hours on night cops. My brain is not good at multitasking.

"Fine," I tell Cindy, who still has the place she got in the divorce settlement.

She says it's fine with her too. By the time I get around to amending my one-word statement, she's headed out the door.

"I'll get my stuff later," are her last words.

I let her go, promising myself I will make it right later, somehow.

I CATCH a break with Heutz. There aren't that many Heutzes in the phone listings, for starters, and when I call the one whose address matches the one Louisa gave me, his wife says he's at work and tells me where.

He answers when I call. Having three people in a row answer the phone when I call them would make this a very lucky day, if it weren't for the fact that the love of my life just walked out the door.

Heutz is willing to answer a few questions about his old friend David Biggio, after I assure him that it's not for attribution.

The main thing Arthur Heutz remembers about their brief reunion is that Biggio seemed a little nervous "like he wasn't all that glad to see somebody from back in the day. I don't know, bad memories I guess. You know, the divorce and all."

Heutz said he didn't recognize him at first, because he'd cut off all his hair.

"Used to have this big mess of dark hair, and now he'd shaved his head, I guess. Bald as a coot."

Biggio told him that he was living across the bridge in Topping, and was working here and there.

"But he said something weird. He told me he'd appreciate it if I didn't tell anybody where he was, or that he had met me. Said he wanted to leave his old life behind.

"He said he might be reconnecting with some of his old acquaintances pretty soon, but that he wanted it to be a surprise."

I thank Mr. Heutz for his time and assure him again that I will not be using his name in print.

The story in the *Post*, the one we more or less reprinted, didn't give the name of the insurance company that sold David Biggio a policy. It didn't name the agency either.

There aren't that many insurance agencies in the Topping metropolitan area though. I'm sure that, if I can get away from the paper for a few hours, I can find the guy who sold Biggio that policy.

I stop by and prepare to sweet-talk Sally Velez, who has already cut me slack within the last twenty-four hours by letting me go home early last night.

"Yeah," she says when I'm less than a paragraph into my plea. "We can spare you. The way the dragon lady's been on us about this story, I can defend paying Chuck Apple to put in some overtime."

I thank her profusely, and by twelve thirty, I'm on my way east.

When I get down there, my first stop is at the hardware store in Kilmarnock that Chopper Ware owns and runs. He doesn't seem all that pleased to see me. Maybe I should have brought Sarah Goodnight along.

I wait for him to discuss carriage bolts and heavy hex nuts with one of the locals for what seems like ten minutes. Even indoors, he wears that damn hat. Then, when I ask him about the life-insurance policy his former tenant took out, and who might have sold it to him, he asks me what the hell business is it of mine.

"The man's dead," Chopper says. "Why can't you all leave him alone?"

I remind Chopper that I am a reporter, which kind of makes it my business, especially when I'm getting my ass handed to me by the *Washington Post*.

Mr. Ware avows that he has no idea who might have sold Biggio life insurance, not a clue in the world. No amount of beseeching on my part moves him.

"Jesus Christ," he says, "the SOB destroyed my plane and turned my life upside down. How about you let me have a little peace."

It's after two o'clock, and I've been living on coffee and Camels so far today. There's a diner not far from Chopper's store.

I order a softshell sandwich with my two favorite vegetables: french fries and mac and cheese.

I get into a conversation with the waitress, a dyed-blonde cutie with what appears to be War and Peace tattooed the length of her left arm. She calls me "honey" and keeps the iced tea coming. When I tell her I'm from the paper in Richmond, she rolls her eyes and says I must be "poking into that Biggio mess."

I admit I am. I tell her that my boss is on my butt because another paper beat us on a story about the life-insurance policy Biggio took out, and now I'm kind of under the gun to try to find the fella who sold it to him.

"Oh," she says, "that'd be Eddie."

Three guys at the booth behind mine chime in.

"Yeah," one of them says, "I bet he rues the day he sold that one," and the other two guys bust out laughing.

They don't even need a newspaper down here. Just like Chopper said, everybody knows what everybody else is up to anyhow. The trick is getting them to share the breaking news with outsiders. Must be my warm, outgoing personality. Or I just got lucky.

I leave a 30 percent tip.

"Eddie" is Eddie Bonner. He runs a one-man agency on the same street as Chopper Ware's hardware store and the diner. When I walk in, a guy with a bad comb-over and a beer gut comes out from behind his desk to greet me.

He loses the smile and lets go of my hand when I tell him who I am and who I work for, but he doesn't show me the door.

"You want to know about that damn life-insurance policy," he says. "Hell, why not? Everybody else does."

"Everybody else," though, does not include the news media, it appears. Once it was known that Biggio took out that half-million-dollar policy, the big boys apparently weren't that interested in talking at length to the guy who sold it to him. Other than the *Post* reporter, he's spoken to no one in the news business.

This one should be on the record. I hold my breath when I start asking questions, hoping he will, by not protesting, let me use his name.

"He just came in here one day," Bonner says, "and tells me he wants to buy a life-insurance policy. He didn't look like he had two cents to rub together, to tell you the truth.

"But when I told him how much it cost, he said it wouldn't be any problem. He said he had come into some money and wanted to take care of his little girl. He said it was in case something happened to him."

The agent asks me if I knew Biggio. I told him I didn't, that I'd seen pictures, but that was all.

"Well, he is, or was, a strange-looking dude. Fierce. He didn't blink much."

Bonner confirms that he sold the policy just fifteen days ago.

"No way in hell he's going to get it though."

"So you think he committed suicide?"

The agent looks me in the eye.

"Let me put it this way. If it was suicide, or even looks like it might have been suicide, the company has a lot bigger lawyers than his little girl does."

There isn't much that's higher on my shit list than an insurance company that takes your check every month and then won't pay out. I have to admit, though, that little Brandy Klassen isn't likely to be getting a check for half a mil anytime soon.

"So he didn't say anything else about how he had 'come into some money'?"

Bonner shakes his head.

As I'm about to leave, another question occurs to me.

"He had to fill out some kind of forms, though, to get the policy?"

"Yeah. Sure. We do like to get it in writing. You know?"

"Was there anywhere on there where he would have been asked to list a contact, like somebody to get in touch with if he happened to fly his plane into a crowded building?"

Bonner looks like he's hesitating. Maybe there's some insurance agents' version of that HIPPA bullshit that keeps the doctor from telling everybody you have the clap.

I remind him that Biggio is dead and certainly isn't going to suffer from him giving me that information.

He turns out to be an accommodating enough fellow, not as predisposed to tell someone with a notepad to go fuck himself as some of his fellow citizens from more jaded climes.

"Yeah," he says. "He had a contact."

I wait for it.

"He put down that guy that owns the hardware store. James Ware. They call him Chopper. I think he was renting from him."

I don't have the inclination right now to return to Chopper's hardware store and ask him about this. It can wait.

I'M BACK by six, in time to take over from Chuck and promise him a free round or two at Penny Lane next time we're both there. I'm sure Rita Dominick will appreciate my saving the company even more hours of overtime by working what will wind up being a fourteen-hour day.

The cops don't seem to have much more on the crash, or at least nothing their flack, my good friend and former newsroom inmate Peachy Love, is willing to share with me.

I call her at home. When she picks up, I hear music and laughter in the background. Peachy apparently slips into a quieter room.

"Wendell's here," she says. "We're having a party. Got some friends over."

I'm kind of glad to hear it. Peachy and I have been known to hook up, and the fact that her longtime long-distance candy man is in town means I probably won't have to make up an excuse not to come over and show her some attention. I'm crazy about Peachy but, present falling-out with Cindy notwithstanding, I don't really want to make my life more complicated than it is already. If Cindy didn't shoot me for slipping around, Wendell, who is a very big man, might pinch my head off and crap down my neck.

She says the cops are still treating it like an accident, although they're about a million miles from closing the books on it. The news about the life-insurance policy has certainly made them rethink things.

Yeah, I remark, it would. What are the odds of buying a half-million-dollar life-insurance policy two weeks before you die?

"The chief is getting a lot of heat, and he's passing it on."

I guess so. The number of dead reached twenty-five today when another poor soul passed away. The story has ceased to be national. There was another nut-job shooting out West, then an oil train spilled and fucked up a river in Minnesota. Like the gal on *Saturday Night Live* used to say, it's always something. I once had a guy who was in the business of rehabilitating reputations tell me that the first thing he always told his clients when they screwed up was that there is almost nothing so horrible or unforgivable that it won't get wiped away in a news cycle or two.

I have enough to push the story forward a little, enough to keep the publisher off my back for another day. I have a little more insight into Mr. Biggio, a pretty good picture of how the insurance deal happened.

I still can't get my mind around it though. What could have made the man angry enough to take out twenty-five strangers with an airplane? I had Sarah check police records all over eastern Virginia, and David Biggio seems to have stayed on the right side of the law for the past few years. There isn't anything to suggest he was about to snap. He was less of a problem after he left Richmond than he was when he lived here.

Mass killings happen all the time, from one end of the country to the other. This one made the NRA folks happy, I'm sure, because for once it didn't involve a nut with a gun he never should have been allowed to own. But Biggio wasn't sending up red flags that anybody saw, or has been willing to talk about. Sure, he had reason to be pissed at his former wife, and maybe at the lawyer who abused him in court during the custody trial. But there's no evidence that he planned any menace toward his wife, and the lawyer didn't work for BB&B. If anything, Biggio was going to make his ex's life easier by passing on the only kind of inheritance he could to their daughter.

All during the evening, I know I should call Cindy. I don't though. It's easier to find anything else to do, to tell myself I'll make it up to her tomorrow.

And, when I'm finally finished, it's much easier to go over to Penny Lane and help close the place down for the night than it is to go home to that big, empty bed.

CHAPTER EIGHT

Friday

As is my custom on Tax Day, I call my accountant and tell her to file an extension. She's always thrilled to hear from me, I'm sure, having nothing else to do on April 15. As usual, I have to converse with one of the minions she brings in this time of year to handle idiots like me.

The young man I speak with is a familiar voice. I've talked with him on at least a couple of other mid-April days.

"The usual, Mr. Black?" he asks. I think I hear him sigh. I tell him I've just been too damn busy to keep Uncle Sam updated on my financial status. He says he hears that a lot.

While it's still pleasantly cool outside, I head back to the scene of the crime. I haven't been there in a few days, and I don't know what I'm expecting to find.

The morbidly curious have thinned out a bit. The wreckage where Dark Star and the building next to it once stood is still there. It might have been bulldozed by now, but L.D. Jones's minions are continuing to do something resembling detective work here. They're mostly going over the place with a fine-tooth comb, looking for what I have no idea. L.D.'s philosophy seems to be that if you can't work smart, work hard.

Across the street, they're replacing the ruins of the 7-Eleven sign that David Biggio's plane clipped off on his way to hell. I walk over there to buy some cigarettes.

There are a couple of guys outside who look like this might be their "third place," as the kids put it. You know: homeless shelter, Monroe Park, 7-Eleven. It's a place where guys with limited means can buy one beer at a time and drink it on the curb, the can ensconced in a paper sack.

The guys would put the bite on me for some change so they can buy a bus ticket to New York, which is code for "bottle of cheap wine," but then I hear a very familiar voice.

"Dude, leave that guy alone. He's my friend. Besides, he ain't got no money. He works for the newspaper."

I swear, the two of them look at me with something that looks suspiciously like pity before they sidle over to another, more promising mark.

Awesome Dude, out renewing old acquaintances on this fine spring day, gives me a high five. Days like this, he sometimes doesn't get back to Peggy's at all, opting for a nostalgia trip to one of the places where he used to sleep before my mother gave him permanent shelter. Awesome is no prize, but he definitely looks better than the guys he's visiting, probably because he does occasionally touch base with civilization.

"The dude that did this, they ought to string him up."

I remind Awesome that pieces of David Biggio's internal organs probably are still in all the rubble across the street.

"Well," he says, "they ought to bring him back so they can kill him again."

With nothing better to do than grasp at straws, I ask Awesome if any of his old associates hanging out here might have been here a week ago, when it all happened.

He walks away and talks to the other two guys, then comes back.

"That one, Cottonmouth, he says he was here, saw the whole thing."

The guy does look a little bit like a snake. He's skinny, old before his time, and wrinkled. He looks like he's about ready to shed his skin. He kind of slithers over, still holding the beer he's been nursing. He probably sees an opportunity to ingratiate himself, even if Awesome has dampened his expectations as to the contents of my wallet.

I give Cottonmouth a couple of dollars to lubricate his memory.

"Yeah," he says. "I seen the whole damn thing. Surprised nobody hadn't asked me about it yet."

Maybe, I'm thinking, they don't see you as a reliable witness.

"I was sittin' on the step here, mindin' my business," he says, stopping to scratch himself. "Next thing I know, I hear this noise, like the end of the world. Before I can do anything, this plane comes right over the top of the building. Like to have hit it. Took out the sign, and then all hell broke loose. I run like a son of a bitch."

I ask him if he remembers anything else, anything at all.

He shakes his head. My two-dollar investment doesn't seem to be paying off. They usually don't.

But then, as I'm turning to walk away, he says, "Wait. There was one thing."

I wait.

"A few minutes before the plane crashed, I saw a plane come over a couple of times, but higher up. I remember watchin' it go by up there, all lazy like it didn't have nowhere in particular to go. Didn't think nothing about it at the time. Might have been the same one, I guess. I hadn't thought about it 'til now."

I nod encouragingly, hoping for more yet from Mr. Cottonmouth.

He says, after pausing for more exploratory scratching, that something else happened in that brief span before Dark Star became a charnel house.

"Something fell," he says.

He says he heard something hit the asphalt hard on the other side of the 7-Eleven parking lot.

"Was goin' to see what it was, but then, you know, I kind of forgot about it, with all the shit happening. But it made a big racket when it hit, like a gunshot or something."

He shows me approximately where he thought the mystery item might have hit. There's so much crap in the parking lot that looking for anything in particular seems like a fool's errand. Actually this whole gambit seems like a fool's errand. Homeless guy hears a plane up there somewhere a few minutes before the crash. He thinks something from above hit the store's parking lot about that same time.

Most of my leads don't bear fruit, but something happens here that reminds me why I keep following them anyhow, just in case.

Among the discarded Big Gulp cups, stamped-out cigarettes, and Hostess CupCake wrappers, I find a piece of plastic, lying against the curb. It isn't much, but I can tell from its shape that it probably used to be part of a cell phone. I find a few other bits and pieces that look like they're related. I pick up a discarded, one-beer paper sack and put the remains in there.

Across the street, I see the city cops and detectives working away. I wonder if I should relay the information I just gleaned from Cottonmouth to L.D. Jones. I think about it some more and decide that L.D. can wait a bit.

I thank my informant, along with Awesome Dude, who says to tell Peggy he'll be home by suppertime.

Cottonmouth has one question for me.

"Do you think I could get some money out of this, if I got a lawyer? I think I got that post-traumatic whatchamacallit."

I tell him I'll check into it.

CINDY DOESN'T answer when I call, and I have to admit to myself that I'm a little relieved. This is a conversation I need to have, but the coward in me makes me want to put it off awhile longer.

There's time to run back home for a beer and a sandwich before work, maybe even a few minutes to stop by and see Peggy, Andi, and little William.

I park back of the Prestwould. Coming around the corner, I see an emergency vehicle in front of the main entrance. This is a sight I see too often, and one that fills me with dread. Many of my friends here are of a certain age, meaning they're older than dirt. The blinking blue light often means I have one less friend. The place where I live is great for retirees who can afford it. There are enough services available that you can literally go out feet first. Hollywood Cemetery is just a few blocks away, next to Oregon Hill, and the joke around here is that you go from the Prestwould to Hollywood.

Unfortunately, sometimes they do.

The EMT folks already seem to have packed up the unfortunate victim, although I can't see who he or she is.

I get past the cluster fuck around the front door and find Clara Westbrook standing in the lobby, talking with some of our neighbors. I am relieved to see her. She is a ray of sunshine who often brightens my cloudiest days. I would miss her greatly.

My relief must show, because she walks over to me slowly, carrying behind her the oxygen tank, her "little buddy."

"They're not getting me yet, Willie. I've still got some bourbon left to drink."

The bell tolls this time, she informs me, for Feldman, aka McGrumpy.

"Gone?"

"I doubt it. They think he had a heart attack or something."

It turns out that McGrumpy was holding court in the lobby, where he seems to spend most of his waking hours. The man has a tendency to talk shit. He usually gets away with it because he's too old to be the recipient of a well-deserved ass whipping.

This time, though, he picked the wrong place to share one of his more repulsive views.

He was yakking about how tired he was of hearing so much about the Dark Star disaster. He told a couple of his neighbors who weren't savvy enough to avoid any extended conversation with him that he thought it wasn't such a bad idea to clean out some of the "riff-raff" once in a while. His low opinion of Dark Star might have harkened back to the Devil's Triangle's unsavory reputation of past years. Or maybe he just wanted to run his mouth.

Clara, who got her information secondhand from one of the men who was there, said he told them that was "what you get for going out and getting drunk and whoring around."

One of Custalow's coworkers happened to be in the lobby at the end. The handyman had a cousin who was a laborer of some kind. The cousin was having a drink or three at Dark Star last Friday afternoon. They were able to identify his remains through dental records.

Mr. Edward Bevans was not amused by McGrumpy's pronouncement and told him so, rather vigorously. A reasonable, decent man would have apologized and done some quick backtracking. But that wouldn't be McGrumpy.

He stood his ground, until the handyman wrapped his hands around his scrawny neck and lifted him off the lobby's marble floor, then dropped him on it before he could choke him to death.

"They said he seemed like he was having some kind of seizure, and they called 911," Clara said. "But he was breathing when they rolled him out."

I told Clara I hoped nearly killing McGrumpy wouldn't get the guy in any serious trouble, although it's hard to imagine things working out that well. I just hope the son of a bitch doesn't die.

"Well," she said, "nobody deserves to be choked right here in the lobby."

She pauses to take in a little more oxygen, then smiles and winks.

"But if anybody did, I suppose it would be Mr. Feldman."

There's a cloud hanging over our fair city since last Friday. Everybody seems a little out of sorts, depressed, maybe scared, which leads to angry. It's a good time to keep your thoughts to yourself, especially if your brain is as full of crap as Feldman's is.

After bolting a sandwich and a beer, then another beer for dessert, I call Kate, who sounds a little less addled than she did a couple of days ago. I ask her if she's filed her taxes, and she says she thinks, or hopes, that her late husband took care of that already.

"Greg was good about that sort of thing," she says. It seems like she chokes a little on his name. I remind her of our unbroken record of not filing on time, and what I hear on the other end sounds almost like a laugh.

She doesn't know anything more about any possible connection between BB&B and the mad bomber than she did the last time we talked. She says she hasn't had time to really look into it. I'm thinking that it probably takes most of Kate's energy right now just to keep herself and Grace fed and clothed.

She says, though, that she is going to call one of the partners who didn't make it to happy hour last Friday and ask him to check around and see if he and his fellow lawyers can think of anybody who might have wanted to kill them.

"Surely," I said, "BB&B has made some enemies over the years."

Most of their work, she reminds me, is corporate, where they use pens and now keystrokes instead of guns or aircraft.

"But I'll check. The partner who wasn't there the day it happened, he's about seventy-five now. He's the closest thing to institutional memory they have."

I ask her if she'd like for me to come over. She says she thinks that might not be a good idea. I have to agree, silently, that she's probably right. I am on the verge of fucking up my best chance lately at future happiness, and a visit to the emotionally vulnerable Kate right now might reduce those chances to zero, if they aren't gone already.

I have time to run by Peggy's just long enough to tell her that her erstwhile tenant will be home for supper, and to find out that Andi is "seeing someone," another VCU student who, while a perfectly fine young man, did not pick his parents as well as the guy who knocked her up.

My daughter has shown no signs of ever walking down any aisle with Thomas Jefferson Blandford V, my grandson's father. I haven't exactly been wishing for a union of the Blacks and Blandfords, but I have to admit that marrying into that old, rich-as-shit Richmond family would solve every money problem Andi and William and probably William's future children could ever encounter.

My mother, incurable romantic that she is, believes firmly in marrying for love rather than money. She never felt the urge to marry the late Artie Lee, my African American father, though.

Somehow she sees her single-mother experience as affirmation of Andi's decision to, so far, go it more or less alone.

"Just look how well you turned out," she is fond of saying.

Indeed.

Our newsroom is buzzing this fine spring day. As is often the case, the buzz is not a happy one, more like what you might hear from a nest of pissed-off hornets. The rumor mill is grinding away. More layoffs, cutbacks, furloughs, and other staples of twenty-first-century print journalism are on the way.

This is how bad it's gotten. Our chain has shut down a couple of smaller dailies in the hinterland, and our outpost has been ridden so hard that we're now praying to be bought by chains we found repulsive not too long ago.

The devil we know, in this case enthusiastically represented by Rita Dominick, has become less palatable than some unknown demon lurking in the shadows. We're opting for Door Number Three.

"You know," Enos Jackson says as we're standing around the coffee pot, "I really miss Grubby."

Ray Long sets down his cup, spilling only a little on the carpet, and starts laughing. Pretty soon, we're all howling. We didn't know how good we had it until our late publisher was cruelly taken from us by a city bus.

The rumors could be rumors, but too often lately whatever the gossip factory churns out becomes sad reality.

After more or less dodging the bullets for the last four years, I'm sure my time is coming. I'm pretty much the whole package: Fifty-six years old, good salary, a well-earned reputation for antagonizing the powers that be, maybe a wee bit of a drinking problem. I'm a human resources ax-wielder's dream.

I used to try to stave off old age. These days I find myself figuring just how many more days and months lie between me and a retirement in which I can afford food, shelter, and medical care.

Wheelie passes the word up to our publisher that we are still bird-dogging the Dark Star story. I've told him about my interview with Mr. Cottonmouth, real name unknown. Neither he nor Ms. Dominick seem terribly impressed with the remembrances of a guy even Awesome Dude finds a bit sketchy.

The part about "something" hitting the ground just before the crash doesn't really titillate anybody, even when I show them the cell phone detritus I found.

"That could have come from anywhere," Dominick says. "Some guy could have dropped it out of his car, or it fell out of his pocket."

I note that it seemed to have fallen pretty hard.

"Well," she says, "I guess that's about the best we can do then." And she turns and walks off.

Wheelie asks me if I've told the cops about the phone yet.

I tell him I haven't, but I probably ought to give L.D. Jones a call to let him know we're mentioning it in tomorrow morning's paper.

I check first with Peachy to see if the cops are onto any of this yet, and she says they aren't. They've been doing their detective work across the street, where the plane actually crashed.

So I call L.D.'s cell. It's after eight, so I'm sure he'll be even less thrilled than usual to hear from me.

"Yeah," he says by way of greeting. "What the hell do you want?"

I can hear the Nationals game in the background. I can imagine my one-time basketball buddy lolling in his La-Z-Boy with a beer at his side. I almost hate to disturb his repose.

"You did what?" he says. I can hear the chair spring up.

I explain again what Cottonmouth told me. L.D. seems torn between threatening me, for the umpteenth time over the years, for interfering with an "ongoing investigation," and trying to discount what my unreliable source told me.

"Well," I say when he stops yelling long enough to catch his breath, "I did find parts of a cell phone. It looks like somebody dropped it a long way."

He's silent for a few seconds. Then he asks me (and asking me anything is like swallowing a razor blade for L.D. Jones) if the police can send someone around to retrieve what he now refers to as evidence.

I tell him that's fine. I ask him to please keep me in the loop if the shattered phone yields anything resembling a break in the case.

He grunts and says he'll keep me in mind.

The cops probably are close to winding up their investigation around Dark Star. I'm pretty sure they will be happy to close the books on it, writing it off as either a horrible accident or the act of a madman. If I weren't going to run the bit about the cell phone in the paper tomorrow, I think L.D. would be pretty happy to pretend I never called him.

I don't make the chief's life easy. That isn't my job. Before I hang up, though, I make an executive decision.

In the story, I tell L.D., we will just say that bits of what appears to be a cell phone were found after an unnamed source who was at the 7-Eleven that day heard something crash to the ground just before the plane hit.

The readers, if they wish, can deduce that the chief's minions stumbled on Cottonmouth themselves.

L.D. understands what I'm saying. He has a lot of trouble, though, with that little two-word phrase expressing gratitude.

"Good," is as far as his vocal chords can stretch. He promises to call me, though, if there are any "significant breaks."

Better than nothing. And my story won't be made any worse by not inserting myself into it. Actually it suits me to write it this way.

A byline and a salary are all the compensation I crave.

Occasionally, if I stick my big schnoz deeply enough into a story, a first-person slant becomes necessary. Mostly, though, the best newspaper pieces are the ones where you aren't aware there's an ink-splattered wretch there, getting between you and the story.

I have to make a couple of trips out to crime scenes before I'm allowed to go home for the evening. A guy turned up dead in an alleyway over in Carver and two teenage gunslingers had at it in the midst of a party on the South Side. If there is any good news out of that one, it's that they only managed to shoot each other, one of them fatally. Two weeks ago, some asshole plugged a little girl drawing on the sidewalk in front of her mom's apartment. She got caught in the crossfire.

I told that story to R.P. McGonnigal and Andy Peroni the other day at Joe's.

"Man," R.P. said, "why do you do what you do? Can't you get a job that doesn't make you want to cry or get drunk?"

I told him somebody has to do it. Otherwise bad people do bad things unnoticed. If I can get some of our readers as pissed off as I am, maybe some good will come of it. As it is, we've come to accept forty or so murders annually as a good year in Richmond. Too many people go with "It's been worse" instead of "It could be a hell of a lot better."

"Besides," I told him, "what the fuck else am I qualified to do?"

My cell phone never rings loud enough unless I'm in, say, a movie theater and forgot to turn it off. When I check it after midnight, I see that Cindy called.

I see that she tried to reach me about ten thirty. I consider giving her a call, then decide I can wait until I'm in a better mood and she's awake.

A better plan seems to be to wander down the street again and join some of my colleagues in helping Penny Lane whittle down its beer inventory.

CHAPTER NINE

Saturday

The local TV news normally consists of teasing out the weather report in drips and drabs between stories that are either inane or took place in some other time zone. If the weekday news is lame, the weekend reports are quadriplegic, usually hosted by what appear to be college students who shop for their on-air clothes at thrift stores.

This time, though, they've got a live one.

"We've just learned," the semibreathless young woman tells us, "of a homicide in Richmond's West End."

She has my attention. I put down the butter knife. Custalow comes in from the kitchen. The street she names is not one on which people usually get killed. It is in a neighborhood where the natives don't understand what's so exotic about *Downton Abbey*.

And then she drops the name.

Thomas Jackson Bonesteel.

"Holy shit," says Custalow. I concur.

He's everybody's favorite get-out-of-jail lawyer. While Marcus Green, now with the assistance of my ex-wife, does occasionally put justice ahead of profits, Jack Bonesteel always has, or had, his eyes on the prize.

He and Marcus seemed to compete to see who could run the cheesiest lawyer ads on TV. The present one for Bonesteel, which I assume we won't be seeing again, includes the baritone punchline: "Unfairly accused? Insurance company won't pay? Creditors on your butt? Tell 'em you know Jack."

And the scowling visage of Jack Bonesteel fills the screen, his bald head gleaming and his arms crossed like an amalgamation of Mr. Clean and a nightclub bouncer. A hammer comes down on what I assume is steel in the background.

He must have been sixty years old at the time of his untimely passing. He had been working for the highest bidder for as long as I can remember. He was disbarred at least once, and he made the news every so often for incidents involving either intimidation or outright assault. Fortunately for him, he was a good lawyer.

He even tried to light me up once upon a time. It was at least fifteen years ago. He was defending a state legislator who was involved in some shady real estate dealings. I was covering the lege at the time and dug up a few things that Bonesteel and his client wanted to stay buried.

He and I happened to be at the same watering hole one night, popular with the pols, lobbyists, and journalists. Bonesteel had, I suppose, imbibed a few bourbons before he spotted me in the crowd. He tried to do that thing he did, getting in your face and promising all sorts of dire retribution "if you don't stop printing lies about my client."

Having also had a few, I told him to go fuck himself. Then I told him that I had no intention of striking an ambulance-chasing scumbag unless the scumbag threw the first punch, which I heartily encouraged him to do, while we had plenty of witnesses. I also told him his breath stunk.

He kept staring at me, trying not to blink. He wasn't a big guy, really, but he seemed big when he got all puffed up with righteous indignation.

Finally he laughed and said, "Ah, you're not worth getting my suit dirty over."

I told him, as he walked away, that if he ever laid a finger on me, I would dirty that suit up so he wouldn't even be able to send it to the cleaners. After that we kind of avoided each other.

The news report doesn't tell me much, just that the body had been there for some time and that the police suspected foul play.

I get dressed and go to the late Mr. Bonesteel's neighborhood. There are police cars everywhere. Shrubbery is being trampled. I fear for the safety of the boxwoods.

Then I spy Gillespie among the horde. He's in major donut debt to me, and I expect a little help once in a while.

He steps behind one of the boxwoods and I follow.

"I can't tell you much," he says, "but this guy was pretty beat up."

"Like how."

Gillespie tells me that the victim had been shot in the groin, both kneecaps, and the stomach. He was gagged, and Gillespie says it's his bet that whoever plugged him left him there to bleed to death.

"He didn't die easy."

I had to admit that maybe even Thomas Jackson Bonesteel might not have deserved to go that way.

"He'd been there awhile," Gillespie says. "Smell was enough to gag a maggot."

"How long?"

"Probably a week or more."

"How come nobody found him until now?"

Gillespie looks around, probably trying to make sure the chief doesn't catch him talking to the enemy.

"He was supposed to be on two weeks' vacation. One of the neighbors noticed the car was still there and then checked and saw that the mailbox was crammed full. She was the one that called 911."

I look around and see Mark Baer. Since this doesn't exactly fall under the auspices of the night cops beat, Sally Velez probably told Baer to get over here, assuming that I would want a few more hours' sleep.

So I share what I know with Baer, who never shares anything with anyone, because that's just the kind of guy I am.

"Where'd you get this?" he asks me. A reliable source within the police department, I tell him.

"I can't use this without a name."

"Then don't use it."

He walks off to verify what I just told him. I'll divulge a little information to Baer if it helps the home team, but I'm sure as shit not going to burn any sources to help the little prick.

At nine fifteen, I call Cindy. She answers and doesn't sound as if I woke her up.

It's only been two days since we parted on less-than-amicable terms. Frankly I've been glad to have a reason to stay busy. I miss her. I tell her that.

"Me too," she says.

I start to explain about Kate and the necessity of staying in touch with her.

"I know. I know. But it's hard, Willie. The asshole (her term of endearment for her former husband) was always slipping around, lying about where he was, which usually was with the bitch he wound up marrying after we split or some other bitch. It's kind of put a dent in my trust reserve. And then when I found out you'd been to see Kate . . ."

I assure her that I know how she feels. I do actually. Not that I was a saint, but my third ex-wife got her panties caught in a wringer a couple of times when I found out that girls' night out included at least one boy.

There is no way to promise her that I won't be in contact with Kate again. As a matter of fact, I need to get back in touch with her today. But what I can do is promise that I won't do anything behind her back. I also promise her that whatever intercourse I have with my ex will definitely not be of a sexual nature.

"I appreciate that," she says. "Damn, Willie. I didn't really think you were reverting to old habits, or old wives. But you worry me sometimes."

I ask her to do something that all three of my former wives might find difficult. I ask her to trust me.

Maybe it's because she doesn't know my whole, sordid track record. Maybe it's because we both want to believe the future will be better than the past.

"OK," she says. "I trust you. So are you doing anything tonight?"

"Other than working, you mean?"

"Oh, yeah. Well, is it OK if I come back and wait up for you?"

I tell her, in all sincerity, that it will be the high point of my day.

"I'll make sure it is," she says.

My next stop, where I doubt I'll be welcomed, is at Louisa Klassen's house. I'm hoping the happy family is back from their brief exile, and that they are not being hounded by my competitors.

There's a car in the driveway and no camera crews parked in the yard. My luck holds when I knock and Louisa answers. She looks like she's had a rough night. She tells me that they didn't get back into town until two A.M. thanks to a big wreck on I-81.

My luck seems a tad more shaky when the tattooed and surly Bobby comes up behind her.

He starts in on me, telling me to get the fuck out of there. But Louisa surprises me by telling him to back the hell off. He surprises me and does what she says.

"This man might be able to tell us about the insurance policy," she tells her husband. The whiff of half a million dollars seems to soothe Bobby a bit.

I tell her that the main obstacle between her daughter and $500,000 is proving that her first husband was just a bad pilot and didn't deliberately crash his plane into a restaurant full of people.

"David wouldn't do that," she says. I try to be as supportive of that contention as I can be. She says they are supposed to meet with the insurance people Monday morning. I advise her to bring a lawyer along. Trying to throw some business his way, I suggest Marcus Green. I even have one of Marcus's cards.

She thanks me.

"I've seen his ads on TV and all. He seems like he could help."

"Yeah," Bobby says. "He's colored and all, but he looks like he could kick some butt."

I'm pretty sure Bobby isn't aware of my mixed-race heritage and is just being your basic asshole racist. Still, I want to kick him in the balls. Later maybe.

So I am allowed inside the front door. The TV is on, and Louisa's daughter, Brandy, is sitting on the couch, deeply involved with the iPad in her lap.

"Brandy, honey," Louisa says, "this is Mr. Black, from the newspaper."

She looks up and shrugs. I don't think the possibility of being a small-time heiress in the near future has her on tenterhooks at present. She's a pretty girl, with dark hair and a long face, but she seems to have picked up some of her stepfather's social graces.

Louisa frowns at the girl, then turns back to me.

"You know," she says, "it's funny you mentioning this Marcus Green. I always have him fixed in my mind with that other fella, the 'tell 'em you know Jack' guy. Oh, you might not have heard, but they found him dead in his house this morning."

I tell her that I know. I tell her I've just come from the scene of the crime.

"No kidding? Wow, it must be exciting. I mean, seeing everything you get to see."

"That's one word for it."

"Well," she says, "I don't want to speak ill of the dead, but he was kind of a pain in the butt. Not a nice man."

"You knew him?"

She looks at me.

"Oh, yeah, I guess I didn't tell you. No reason to. But he was the lawyer we hired when we were getting full custody rights."

She lowers her voice a little, although Brandy seems to be in a world of her own.

"We spent a ton, and it took us years to pay it off. He threatened to sic the bill collector on us."

I am taken aback. Thomas Jackson Bonesteel, whom somebody apparently killed in a highly personal fashion sometime in the last ten days or so, is the guy who managed to take David Biggio's only child away from him and humiliate him in the process.

It hardly seems worth mentioning to Louisa Klassen that it would be very interesting to know where her late ex-husband was around the time someone was using Bonesteel for target practice.

Amazingly it's the seemingly dimwitted Bobby who catches on first.

"You don't think he killed this guy too?"

I note that anything's possible.

"Wow," Bobby said. "That guy really didn't like lawyers."

We part on somewhat amicable terms. I tell Louisa I will keep her informed when I know anything and wish her and Bobby good luck with the insurance piranhas on Monday. They're going to need it.

KATE, WHEN I call, says she's heard about Bonesteel. She says she has no knowledge of him ever working for or with BB&B.

"He's not exactly their kind of lawyer, if you know what I mean. Way too rough around the edges."

"Says the woman who's partnering with Marcus Green."

"Hey, don't even mention Marcus in the same sentence with that jerk. Marcus actually does some good once in a while."

She also says she has contacted the veteran partner, and he has promised to get back with her.

"He lost more people at Dark Star than I did, and I guarantee you he will do whatever he can to find out if there's any connection there."

I tell her about the Bonesteel-Biggio connection.

"Wow. Well, I don't think the cops will have a hard time figuring that one out. But why the hell did he have to follow that up by killing a whole bar full of lawyers, including my husband?"

If I knew the answer to that one, I could sit down and start writing instead of chasing my tail.

Baer is back at the paper by the time I get in at two. He's already written his story. I don't like much about Mark Baer, but I do have to admire his work ethic. He doesn't let the fact that the *Washington Post* hasn't, for some odd reason, scooped him up yet dampen his enthusiasm for his chosen line of work.

A friend at the *Post* told me last year, over drinks at the state press association award-fest, that Baer keeps applying. He said he thought he was trying too hard.

Baer was able to get someone to confirm what Gillespie told me, and he seems so damn smug about it that I almost don't tell him about Bonesteel being Louisa Klassen's lawyer in the custody battle.

"He was her lawyer? Good God!"

I tell him that he's going to have to share a byline on this one. I didn't spend part of my morning visiting the lovely Klassens so I could make Baer look better. What we finally agree on is that Baer will write the lede and I'll write a sidebar on the Biggio connection. He'd like it all for himself, but I have some quotes and other information from my visit that I'll be sharing with our readers instead of Mr. Baer.

Wheelie seems pleased that we will have something the TV news folks don't have, but he seems a little distracted.

He calls me aside.

"Have you seen an iPhone around here anywhere?"

I ask him to be more specific. There is hardly a minute when I don't hear somebody's personalized ringtone going off somewhere in the newsroom.

"Rita has lost her phone. She's pretty sure she had it when she came to the newsroom earlier today, and now she can't find it. She thinks somebody might have stolen it."

That seems to be a pretty rash statement, I opine. First off, just about everybody in the newsroom already has an iPhone. Other than me, it might be 100 percent. Second, why the hell would you steal somebody else's phone, even if you didn't have one?

Wheelie shrugs.

"The information on it? E-mail messages and such? Or maybe somebody was just pissed off."

OK. That's a possible motive. With more suit-generated shit headed down the drain toward us peons, I can see that.

Still it seems like a stretch.

"Well," Wheelie says, "I can guarantee that we won't hear the last of it until that phone's found."

No doubt.

"You remember that scene in 'The Caine Mutiny,' where Humphrey Bogart is going batshit because somebody stole the strawberries? Well, insert iPhone for strawberries."

I nod and tell Wheelie I will keep an eye out for wayward iPhones.

I do call L.D. Jones about three to let him know about the connection, but only after I've finished the story and gotten another couple of quotes from Louisa Klassen.

"Why do you keep calling me with this crap?" the chief says in lieu of "Thank you." "You're ruining my digestion."

I suggest more fruits and vegetables. He suggests something else.

"In light of this, it seems there might be some indication that Biggio didn't like lawyers," I note.

He tells me to let the police do the policing.

The evening passes without enough mayhem to send me out of the office. Our front page is pretty much filled up with news of the apparent murder of one of our more outlandish ambulance chasers.

So I have time to actually think a little. The timing of Bonesteel's death is obviously a big link in the chain, what with the Biggio factor. I wonder if the police have any better idea of when he died.

It is highly unlikely that I will be getting this information from L.D., unless it's at a press conference with every TV station in town in attendance.

So I call Peachy. She sounds a little down. Her main man has left again. He seems to stop by for a few days and then move on. A cynic would suspect that he has one in every port, a theory I am not ready to try out on Ms. Love. Hell, maybe she likes the hit-and-run type.

I ask her if the police have any better idea of when Bonesteel died. She surprises me by answering in the affirmative. Somebody's been working hard for a Saturday.

"The way I hear it," she says, "is that one of his ex-wives tried to call him the morning of the sixth, two days before that plane crashed. She said she called early, like seven. Something about late alimony payments—you know about that, Willie. She said she had to catch him early or not at all. Nobody answered. She said he was always at home that time of day. She tried a few more times the next few days and then found out he was supposed to be on vacation."

"OK. So he didn't answer his phone early the morning of the sixth. What does that tell you?"

"His iPhone was still there this morning. The cops were able to check, and the last call he made was at, let's see, 10:17 P.M. on the fifth."

"So you figure he met his maker something between 10:17 that night and seven the next morning."

Peachy congratulates me on my detective skills.

"It's the best we can do for now," she says. "He might have gone out for breakfast, but the ex-wife says he has been good about returning calls, despite his apparent aversion to writing alimony checks, and nobody returned these."

I thank Peachy profusely and find a way to gracefully decline her offer to come over for a drink. I'm hoping that my line to police information L.D. Jones doesn't want to share will not be jeopardized by my reticence.

"Oh, yeah. You got your sweetie waiting for you back home, don't you?"

I tell her that I'm about one misstep away from screwing up my future happiness.

"Well," she says, "we don't want to do anything to get in the way of true love."

When I get home about one A.M. and open the front door, I find a shoe, then another shoe, followed by a blouse, followed by a skirt, leading down the hall. Cindy's panties are the last item I see as I walk into the living room.

"Abe's staying with his girlfriend tonight," the girl of my dreams says, wearing nothing but dimples and a birthday suit remarkably unwrinkled by age. "I thought I'd get comfortable."

With the blinds open on all our sixth-floor windows and all Richmond down below, free to look up if they care, we get very comfortable indeed.

CHAPTER TEN

Sunday

We wake up on the couch, with the sun streaming in. We are sore and stiff and quick to realize that doing the horizontal hula on anything other than a nice, comfy mattress is less appealing in our fifties than it was in our twenties.

"Still," Cindy says, "it's worth the effort."

"Do not go gently into that soft bed."

"Whatever. Get dressed. I don't know when Abe's coming back."

Actually, I tell her, Custalow's meeting us at Joe's for breakfast, along with her brother, Andy, and R.P. McGonnigal. After a night of traction-inducing bliss with Andy's sister, Cindy and I endure the usual bad jokes and innuendos.

Only Custalow is aware of our little mini separation, and Abe doesn't tell tales. He just seems glad that we're back together.

The Dark Star debacle is Topic A here, and probably everywhere else in the region. This morning's paper, chronicling the messy death of a prominent legal eagle and reporting on his connection to David Biggio, is being used for more than lining the parakeet cage. I saw three different patrons reading either A1 or the turn page as we walked back to our table.

"Any chance the guy didn't kill this Bonesteel character too?" McGonnigal asks. I can feel the party at the next table's ears turn in our direction.

I tell them all, and anyone else who's listening, that I'm not even sure Biggio deliberately crashed the plane yet, and I don't know where he was when everyone's least-favorite mouthpiece was murdered.

"Aw, bullshit," Andy says. "You know he did it. Can't be any other way. He hated lawyers, and this guy took his little girl away from him."

All the same, I caution against haste. I still have a couple of things to check, I tell my dubious friends and eavesdroppers.

Sunday's one of my two days off. Yeah, right. With Baer and who knows else snooping around, trying to figure this one out, I'm forgoing my day of rest.

I drop Cindy off with a heartfelt promise to take her to dinner somewhere nice tonight, someplace where the entrées can run into double figures.

"Big spender," she says, kissing me good-bye as I drop her off at the front door.

I've probably tapped Peachy Love for all the information I can for a little while, but there's one other possibility.

I drive down Broad, turn right on Lombardy, and am soon in the area where I know Gillespie's patrolling this lazy spring afternoon. I peruse the parking lot at the Sugar Shack and—what are the odds?—there's his patrol car.

I park on the other side of the lot, slip inside, and order a dozen donuts. Then I walk over and tap on his window, holding my bait in front of me. He's got half a chocolate-glazed in his mouth. I motion for him to unlock the other door. He frowns but does it, as helpless as a beagle facing a slice of bacon. Plus, it's so boring here on a Sunday afternoon that he probably is glad for the company, although I doubt he'd admit that.

"My gift to the precinct," I tell him. I wonder how many will be left by the time Gillespie reports back tonight.

We talk a little guy sports talk, and then I ask him if there's anything new cooking on the Dark Star case, other than the Bonesteel connection.

He swallows and wipes some crumbs off his chin.

"Nothing, except the cell phone."

"You mean, the stuff I found over at the 7-Eleven?"

"Nah. I mean the call."

"The call?"

"Yeah. The call to the plane. I thought the chief had already put that out."

I assure Gillespie that that's the case, and I just haven't checked my e-mail yet, this being Sunday.

"So, what call?"

The Sugar Shack's most reliable patron seems a little hesitant. Finally, though, rightly figuring that I'll suss this one out anyhow, Gillespie tells all, bless his heart. As always, I didn't hear it from him. He even tells me to scrunch down in the seat, so no one will see him consorting with the enemy.

Less than three minutes before the plane crashed, Gillespie tells me, someone made a call to Biggio's cell phone, the same one I assume I found pieces of in the parking lot.

"What did he say? What did the other person say?"

Gillespie eyes the dozen donuts calling his name.

"Nobody knows that. But somebody checked the phone records, and they can see that there was a call."

"Just three minutes before the crash."

"Yeah. They can tell it was short. About ten seconds, I think."

I ask Gillespie whom the call came from.

"It was one of those damn throwaways, the ones the drug dealers use."

I'm digesting this while Gillespie digests the donut he's been eyeing. Somebody called Biggio, in the plane, three minutes before he did his kamikaze number, and then hung up—or Biggio hung up—ten seconds later.

WTF.

I promise Gillespie that his name will never be tied to this. The chief's e-mail is probably in my basket already anyhow, I tell him. Bullshit. If I know L.D. Jones, there will be a last-minute press conference tomorrow morning, just in time for a couple of TV news cycles to have it before we go to press.

I wish my source "bon appétit" and walk back to my car.

It's a nice Sunday. A drive to the Chesapeake might be just the thing.

I call Cindy and ask her if she wants to go for a ride. I pick her up and head east.

On the way to Topping, she tells me the latest on Feldman, passed on to her by Clara Westbrook. He is out of the hospital. Apparently he just had a panic attack, brought on by Edward Bevans's attempt to strangle him. I imagine Feldman will live to be 100. Too mean to die.

He's not going to press charges, which surprises me. McGrumpy is nothing if not vindictive. Maybe he fears retribution. But Custalow has already told me there's no way he can save Bevans's job. Abe says he'll give him a good reference. Hell, it beats jail for assault and battery, even if it was justified.

"Am I your sidekick now," Cindy asks me, "your junior detective?"

I remind her that I'm just an honest journalist, not some gumshoe packing heat.

"I don't know," she says, reaching over and giving me a little tug. "It feels like you might be armed and dangerous."

I tell her that if she doesn't stop, I'll have to get out the handcuffs.

The odds of getting decent information in Topping or Kilmarnock on a Sunday are pretty damn long, but anything I do get will give me a one-day head start on everybody else.

We go to the convenience store where Biggio was supposed to be working. There's a woman behind the counter and no customers. Her name is Greta, and she looks like I might have disturbed her beauty sleep. She has an accent from somewhere on the far side of Europe. When I ask her, she says she came here from Serbia. She has a cousin here who was able to get her into the land of the free.

Yes, she says, she knew Biggio. They'd worked together for more than a year. What I'm looking for, I tell her, is some information on how he spent the fifth and sixth.

"Well," she says, stretching and probably glad just to have somebody to talk to, "he work same shifts every week. Never changed."

She walks back to the office and comes out with a weekly schedule.

"His days were—what is the word?—weird."

"How so?"

"So he work late shift on Tuesdays, then work early shift on Wednesdays. Out at eleven, back in by seven. Boss wants us here by six forty-five on early shift, to open doors you know. Shiny-tailed and bushy-eyed, he says."

She says "says" like you'd pronounce "say" with an "s" on the end, not like "sez." It's kind of endearing. Actually Greta's a little endearing. The smart money sez she will have a local husband and an Anglo last name before much longer.

I compliment her on her English. She shrugs and tells me she learned it all from American television. Hell, next time I come down, she'll probably have a Valley Girl accent.

So I'm doing the math. It would take Biggio more than an hour to get to Richmond, and another to get back.

But Greta has one more bit of information.

"He is lucky though. He has a friend, lives just down the street. He stays there on Tuesday nights."

She has the friend's name and address. Marina Jacobs. I'm hoping she won't be too shy to admit that she was apparently sharing a bed with Mr. Biggio.

Ms. Jacobs is working in her garden out back when we park in front of the little frame house. Cindy and I walk around to where she's planting some tomatoes and bell peppers.

"Might be a little early," she says, "but I don't think we're gonna get another frost."

I eschew subterfuge and tell her right off the bat what I'm here about, and that, no, I am not the police, just a reporter.

"Well," she says, putting down the spade she's been using to loosen up the soil, "no points for that. I like cops a hell of a lot better than the media."

I tell her there's a lot of that going around.

She looks to be maybe fifty, which would make her about six years older than the late Mr. Biggio. She looks like she's about to cry.

I promise her that I won't use her name, but that it is important that I can document exactly where Biggio was the night and morning of the fifth and sixth. I tell her about the lawyer who was probably killed back in Richmond during that time frame.

"Nah," she says. "He wasn't in Richmond, I can tell you that. Not unless I'm a lot heavier sleeper than I think I am."

"So he was here all night."

"Sleeping like a baby," she says, then smiles a little. "Well, mostly sleeping."

She says he was good to her, although a little bit strange, given to moods.

"He said he had a family, back in Richmond, but that they weren't on speaking terms. He talked about his little girl a lot. Said they wouldn't let him visit her."

She sighs.

"He had his spells, I guess you'd call 'em, but when he was on his meds, he was OK. I couldn't believe it when I heard what he did. Didn't nobody much around here know we were, you know, seein' each other, maybe Greta and one or two others. So nobody's come around, except you. And I wish Greta hadn't told you."

I tell her again that her name will not appear in print. What I don't tell her is that, when this runs in tomorrow's paper, everybody will be looking for the unidentified woman, and pretty soon she will be identified. Guess that makes me either a rat bastard or a good journalist, if there's any difference.

Cindy's studying her garden and telling her she wishes we could have one, but we live in a sixth-floor condominium.

After I think I've learned everything I can from Marina, I thank her for her time and hope I don't wind up making her think even less of "the media" than she already does.

On the way back, I break the news to Cindy that I'm going to have to go in and write a story on one of my two days off, which might put a damper on our dinner plans. It'll be five thirty when we get back, and by the time I write what has to be written today, who knows what time it'll be? With all the unnamed sources in this hot potato, Wheelie and Rita Dominick will probably want to get our lawyer to vet it, if they can find him on a Sunday and he's sober enough to read. In any case, it could be a long night.

"So it looks like I'll be ordering delivery from the Robin Inn again," she says, looking out the window.

"You still owe me a dinner though."

"Absolutely. And at least you had a nice day on the Chesapeake."

"Yeah, I think I saw it when we went over the bridge."

I make a detour to Chopper Ware's place, which gives Cindy the best water view she's had so far, but Chopper's big-ass truck is nowhere in sight, and no one answers when I knock. I have quite a few questions for Mr. Ware, but they can wait, for now.

"Who are you looking for?" Cindy asks. I tell her about David Biggio's landlord.

West Point hardly smells at all when we drive past, and the trip back passes pleasantly, considering that I've just downgraded Cindy's dinner from white tablecloth to pizza box.

I drop her off for the second time today in front of the Prestwould.

"Is it always going to be like this?" she asks as she gets out and walks around my Honda to the driver's side.

"Well, they're getting ready for another round of layoffs. I might soon have lots of time to spend with you."

"I just wish there was some zone there between working seven days a week and going on welfare."

There usually is, of course, but guys who let their beats go fallow for a couple of days when the heat's on sometimes wind up without beats, especially if they're in the Fatal Fifties—too young to retire, too old to outwork or underbid the damn millennials and their younger siblings. See: Mark Baer.

I tell her for about the fourth time in the last twenty-four hours how glad I am to have her back in my world, lean up to give her a kiss, and head back to the office.

I called Sally on the return trip to give her the CliffsNotes version of what I'm going to write. She agrees that people above our pay grade are going to want to see this one.

When I get off the elevator, the newsroom seems to be somewhat unsettled for a Sunday night. That's usually the time when you can get away with bringing your dog in to keep you company.

Sally sees me and calls me over.

"It's that goddamn cell phone," she says.

Apparently Ms. Dominick's precious iPhone hasn't shown up yet. She has been grilling anyone unlucky to be working tonight about it.

"She's sure somebody stole it, for whatever the hell reason."

The publisher sees me. When she comes over, I think it's to talk about what surely will be our lede story on A1 tomorrow.

Instead, she starts asking me about the missing phone. She actually has a couple of spring interns more or less turning the place upside down.

"It's got to be here," she says, looking at me as if I could somehow make it appear.

"Do you want to hear about the story?" I ask.

"What story? Oh, yeah. Let's hear what you've got."

Lovely Rita doesn't really know shit about print journalism, beyond how to sell ads, and our ad department isn't doing diddly with that right now either. If it weren't for the paid obits, we'd be in deeper doo-doo than we already are. Our faithful subscribers' families pay for a nice two-column sendoff for mom or dad when they cancel the subscription.

The chain that owns us seems to show no signs of replacing our erstwhile publisher though. The suits are just cooling their heels, waiting for somebody to offer a decent price for our rag. They'll let the new owners pick their own publisher, and Rita Dominick will be sent somewhere else to torture some other newsroom.

We go into Wheelie's office and get him on the speaker phone. I spell out what I know that I didn't know yesterday and that nobody else with a printing press seems to know yet.

One, somebody called Biggio on his cell phone for a ten-second chat about three minutes before he crashed the plane. The cops have that and probably will disseminate it to the rest of the newshounds tomorrow morning. No, there was no e-mail from L.D. Jones in my inbox. What a shock.

Two, there doesn't seem to be any way that Biggio could have been in Richmond at the time that Thomas Jackson Bonesteel was murdered, if the cops have the times right.

"But you can't name your sources for either one of those?" Wheelie asks. I can hear kids screaming and the TV in the background. I'm kind of screwing up Wheelie's day off, it seems.

I make it as clear as I can, to both him and the publisher, that I don't reveal my sources. Ever.

"Well," Dominick says, "then you've got to tell us who the sources are."

I hold out as long as I can. I can count on Wheelie not to blab. With our publisher, the trust is definitely not there.

Finally, though, I compromise. I give them Marina Jacobs's name, threatening them both—as much as you can threaten your bosses—with retribution if her name gets out. I tell them that I absolutely cannot give them my police source's name. For the price of a few donuts, Gillespie is way too valuable to burn.

Wheelie convinces our publisher that we should do it this way. He points out to her what she already should know: my sources are damn good—too good to fuck up.

We put it on the website at eleven, although I'd rather wait and let everybody get it fresh in the paper in the morning.

I would like to be a fly on the wall when L.D. Jones picks up his paper tomorrow.

CHAPTER ELEVEN

Monday

No need to set the alarm. I get a call from the city desk at seven thirty. The chief has called a press conference for nine. He will not be in a very good mood, I'm guessing, since the punch line of his little meeting is in the headline atop A1 this morning: *Mystery call made to death pilot?*

I tell the early morning guy that I'll get it. No need for him to send Mark Baer to do a little beat-poaching, even if it is my day off.

I wouldn't miss this press conference for the world.

Our mouthpiece in charge of saving us from lawsuits didn't do much violence to my story, and the copy desk didn't mangle it. To make sure of that, I was there breathing my nicotine breath down Ray Long's neck while he worked on it. It's all there, spelled out for our readers. The call to David Biggio, plus the fact that Biggio seems to have been occupied elsewhere when his favorite lawyer was murdered.

It was ten thirty when I got back last night. Cindy ordered me a sausage pizza, which I reheated in the microwave and consumed while I filled her in on the story, plus the all-consuming mystery of the publisher's iPhone.

"She must be a piece of work," was Cindy's astute assessment.

She complimented me on eschewing Penny Lane for a change. I didn't tell her how tempted I was when the usual crowd tried to enlist me. Probably, if I'd stayed around much longer, they would have broken down my meager resistance.

Instead, I told her that I loved her more than beer. She seemed touched.

Cindy's already dressed when I make my way out of the bedroom. Exams are looming. Some find it amusing that my girlfriend and my daughter will be graduating, God willing, at the same time, about four weeks from now. Talk about a win-win. Andi's off the payroll, and Cindy's already looking for full-time employment. Soon I'll be so rich I can afford to trade in my Honda before it achieves antique status.

"Good story," she says, munching a bagel while she pours herself and me some orange juice.

I tell her that I'm on my way to find out whether the chief approves of it or not.

The press conference is more sparsely attended than it would have been if everybody didn't already know what L.D. was going to say. There are a couple of TV crews here though.

The chief arrives five minutes after nine. He looks around and sees me in his small audience. He doesn't wave or smile.

He then proceeds to spend the first three minutes or so of his press conference excoriating "so-called journalists" who run stories with "bogus" sources and hinder the police in their efforts to do their job.

"This story," he says, holding up the paper and giving us a free plug, "is rife with inaccuracies."

I raise my hand. He ignores me. After he's ranted for another half-minute, I throw decorum to the wind.

"Would you mind enlightening us on exactly what is inaccurate in the story, Chief?" I yell out when he stops talking long enough to breathe. "I'd like to know so we can correct it."

He points out that the call to Biggio's cell was made two minutes and thirty-seven seconds before the crash, "not three minutes." He points out that it is mere speculation that the pieces of cell phone found in the 7-Eleven lot were from Biggio's phone.

I wait for more. There is no more.

"That's it?"

He would like, I think, to take a running start and try to kick my ass right here in front of the precinct. Then he remembers that he is on TV. He straightens his tie and says the department will be considering what legal action it might take against me and my paper. I smile and thank him for giving us a shout-out.

There's nothing much else for Larry Doby Jones to say that hasn't already been in print. The camera crews are sticking around now to see if the chief and I are going to come to blows. He says something to one of his underlings and then leaves. The underling comes up to me and says, "The chief wants to see you. Right now." Like he's talking to some fifth-grader who's been caught smoking in the boys' room.

"If the chief wants to see me," I advise the guy, "he has my phone number. Tell him to call me and we'll set something up."

He moves in close. The camera crews are packing up now that the chief has left.

"Don't fuck with me," he says. He's some knucklehead whom I've seen around for years, lucky to have a job where he can shine the chief's shoes instead of walking a beat.

I ask him to repeat what he said, so I can be sure I have the quote right. I ask it loudly enough that it gets the attention of a couple of the TV types, who start to come over, smelling great footage for the noon news. The guy walks away, giving me one more glare for the road.

Five minutes later, the chief does indeed call.

"When I find out where you're getting this shit," he promises me, "somebody's going to be out of a goddamn job."

The prudent thing for me to do probably is not to be seen with Gillespie anytime soon.

I jog L.D.'s memory.

"You were going to let me know when something important happened, remember?"

"We had a press conference set up for this morning."

"Yeah. You time these damn things so everybody else gets the word out before we do."

"Well, you can kiss my ass if you think you're ever going to get a tip from me again."

I remind the chief that the number of tips he's ever given me could easily be counted on one hand, sans thumb.

"I guess I'll just have to do the best I can with my own resources," I tell him.

He says he's considering having me arrested for interfering with an ongoing investigation.

I tell him to consider away. He hangs up.

So I'm already semi-pissed off when I stop by the office. This is the day I was really, really not going to work for free, and yet here I am.

My mood lightens somewhat when Sally Velez tells me what has transpired in my absence this morning.

"They found the iPhone."

"Thank God. Our long nightmare is over. Where?"

"That's where it gets good."

Sally is giggling, something she does about once a decade.

It turns out that one of the features department women went to use the facilities and reported a clogged toilet.

"So they got a plumber over here, maybe half an hour ago. And guess what they found when they dug deep?"

Now I'm grinning.

"Oh, no. This is too fucking good."

"Yeah. It must have slipped out of her slacks when she was on the can."

"Has anyone told Dominick yet?"

Sally says she had the honors.

"It was almost as good as a raise."

"What'd she say?"

"Not much. I was trying to keep from busting out laughing. I just told her that they had found a cell phone clogging up one of the toilets in the women's restroom and wondered if it could be hers.

"She said she didn't think that was possible, but when I described it, she got real quiet. Then she said 'shit' and hung up."

I conjecture that this will be the end to the all-out manhunt to find the phone-pilfering culprit.

Sally's smile fades.

"It might not be the best time to gig her about it though. Word is, today's the day they take out the chain saw again."

Well, we knew it was coming. Every time the grim reaper wanders through the newsroom, the survivors breathe a sigh of relief, then wait for the next visit. It never ends. The consultants have been more diligent and invasive than usual the last month, which always bodes ill for the working class.

Sandy McCool, Rita Dominick's administrative aide, got the word out on the q.t., and Sandy is seldom wrong. Nothing to do but wait for the worst.

The way it always goes is that you get a call from Sandy, telling you that you're wanted for a meeting in HR. Might as well pack up your pens and notepads right then. They walk you back to your desk after you find out how big your going-away gift from the company is—lately, a couple of weeks' salary is about it—so you can collect your shit and go.

Because there are no secrets in a newsroom, the great majority of our staff is in the office by eleven.

They don't start the executions until one, and then there seems to be one about every twenty minutes. That's approximately how long it takes to spell it out and deal with the cursing and/or pleading that follows the news that you're screwed.

By four, we know of six fellow employees who are now former employees. Three of them are my age or older. Two of the six are from our copy desk, because who needs people to ensure that all the words are spelled right or that the facts are, in fact, facts? Who needs institutional memory?

I think the bloodletting is over, but then it gets a little worrisome. A couple of people, a woman in features and one in sports, come back to tell us their hours have been cut.

And then the bell tolls for me. I answer, hoping the call is from outside the building. It isn't.

"Willie," Sandy McCool says, her voice giving away just the hint of a tremble, "they need to see you in HR."

I've rehearsed this moment many times. I've seen it happen to so many of my friends and acquaintances. You want to leave with your head up, maybe have something light and pithy to say. "Go fuck yourself, you money-grubbing pigs" is so overdone.

Still when the moment comes, the legs are a bit shaky. The mind gets a little fuzzy. Some of your wittier responses to seeing your future greatly diminished fly from your brain, only to return after you're out the door with a cardboard box full of memories.

I walk into the conference room where the human sacrifices are made. The fear and loathing left by my predecessors seem to foul the air.

Rita Dominick and some goon from HR, apparently here because he's big enough to keep us from strangling the publisher, sit at a table, looking all grim, like they give a shit about my future happiness.

I sit across from them and ask for a blindfold and a cigarette. Nobody smiles.

"Oh, right. No smoking."

"Willie," Ms. Dominick says, "we've had to make some changes."

Oh, hell.

She goes on to tell me what I know already. Circulation's down. Advertising's down. The big guys in corporate are demanding a bottom line every month that is impossible to reach with our current payroll.

I clear my throat.

"So, I guess a raise is out of the question."

The HR goon kind of snorts. Lovely Rita gives him a dirty look.

"I'm glad you still have your sense of humor," she says, turning to me.

"Like Jimmy Buffett says, if we couldn't laugh, we'd all go insane."

I do make the case that she's talking to the person who has had the most A1 stories in our rag over the past year. I know, because Dominick started having somebody keep a count, and the numbers got leaked to the newsroom.

"Well, of course you would. Your beat makes that almost inevitable."

Being a master of making a bad situation worse, I really do seriously consider going over the table and throttling her, but the HR guy probably would spoil my fun before I did any real damage. It would be useless to point out that the guy from whom I inherited night cops basically just wrote his stories from cop press releases. It also would be useless to add that, before I got kicked off the statehouse beat, I probably led the league in A1ers there too.

When the deck is stacked, it's stacked. When you're fucked, you're fucked.

"So, is this where you give me the door prize and Bubba here escorts me on the walk of shame?"

The publisher shakes her head.

"No door prize, Willie. Not that I don't want to can your ass and give you two weeks' severance. I've let people go today who I think a hell of a lot more of than I do you. But the consultants thought we should keep you on, for some reason."

I start to ask her why I'm here, then, other than to be the object of mental torture. But she cuts me off with a very weighty word: However.

"However," says Ms. Dominick, "we are cutting some hours, so we can save some jobs."

The bottom line is that I now will be paid for thirty hours work a week. It's just enough to keep my health insurance, and just enough to discourage me from doing the full kiss-my-ass, you-can't-do-that-to-me monte.

I inquire as to how we are going to keep on top of the Dark Star story if I'm only in for thirty hours a week.

"Well," the publisher says, "we're hoping you can wind this up pretty quickly, so you can get back to your real job, night police. And we can always have Mark Baer take some of the load off you."

I am sure she knows I would work for free to keep Baer from nosing into this story. So now that's what I'll probably be doing. With three days off instead of two, I'll have ten hours I didn't have before to dig deep into the how and why of the city's worst tragedy in decades. The only thing is, I'll be digging for free.

"I'll let you know if I need any help," is about the best I can do in terms of snappy comebacks. Dominick smiles. She knows I'll drop this story when hell freezes over.

Yes, the tendency is to just punch the clock from here on out. Let L.D. Jones feed me crap handouts and spend my so-called off hours supporting our local taverns.

But an old editor told me something once that has stayed with me.

I had been passed over for a promotion, in my early days at the paper. That's it, I told my mentor. All they get from now on is what they pay for.

The old guy sighed and told me to sit down. He reached into his desk drawer and pulled out a bottle of Early Times. He poured us each a double shot's worth in Styrofoam cups.

"Willie," he said, "at the end of the day, is that what you want? Do you want to say, 'I showed them. I didn't work one second more than what I was paid for. They didn't get anything off me.'

"That's the path to mediocrity, Willie. Sometimes you got to work for yourself."

When it's all over, Ms. Dominick reaches across to shake my hand. I almost take it. I stop in time, say, "I'd rather not," turn, and walk out. I won't say my head was high, but for once I thought of the right move in a timely fashion.

As I'm seeing myself out, I do think of one other thing.

"Oh," I say, as I'm closing the door, "I heard the good news. About your iPhone. I can't believe you can get one of those things down a toilet."

The HR guy, who hasn't heard the story yet, looks at her. I leave before she changes her mind and takes away the last thirty hours of my livelihood.

There's a crowd waiting when I get back.

Sarah Goodnight catches on first when she sees there's no goon escorting me.

She gives me a hug.

"You're safe!"

I shake my head.

"Not exactly."

I fill her and the others who've gathered around my desk in on my new, streamlined workweek.

"Well," she says, "that sucks. But at least you're still here."

She says she'll be able to do some of the legwork, if it's needed, on Dark Star. I do have to admit that I prefer her legwork to Baer's. I tell her I appreciate it.

"Maybe we can make another trip down to Topping," she says.

I tell her that's exactly what I have in mind for tomorrow, my third off day in a row that won't be off at all.

I spend the next couple of hours calling the people who weren't as lucky as me. The ones my age just saw the last decent-paying job they'll ever have snatched away by the suits.

It would be in bad taste for me to carp about the loss of one-quarter of my income. My beer glass is, after all, still three-fourths full. With a couple of hours to reflect, I realize that I want to kick the shit out of the Suits Who Never Get Fired not for me but on behalf of my fallen comrades. I'm only dealing with a flesh wound.

I CALL Cindy and give her the news. She suggests that I come home so we can go somewhere to celebrate.

I ask her if she really thinks "celebrate" is the right word.

"You're still working," she says. "You've got your health. You've even got your health insurance. Things could be worse."

I wait until I get home to tell her how much it means to be sharing a bed with someone whose default facial expression is a smile.

Before I leave, I make a call to Topping.

Chopper Ware surprises me by answering.

I tell him we should talk. He asks why. I mention the fact that he's listed as the contact on the late David Biggio's life-insurance policy, indicating a certain intimacy. For a guy who wasn't all that close to his tenant, Chopper apparently was highly esteemed by the deceased.

"Hell," Ware says, "he probably didn't have anybody else to put on that insurance form. His family had pretty much given his ass the deep six."

I persist. There are other questions I have that Chopper might be able to help me with. Like who calls a guy in a stolen plane just before he crashes the plane into a crowded bar? Who else knew Biggio other than Ware? Obviously since the deceased was a friend with benefits to at least one area resident, there was more to the man's life than has been laid out for me so far.

Finally, Ware says I can come tomorrow.

"Be there early," he says. "I ain't got all day to wait for no damn reporter."

He has one more request.

"You might bring that pretty girl back with you."

I tell Sarah, on the way out, that I'll pick her up at seven.

CHAPTER TWELVE

Tuesday

Lemaire is where you go when you want to do it up right. The waiters know their stuff, the silverware's clean, the food's good, and the setting, inside the old Jefferson Hotel, kind of screams out luxe.

It is, in other words, the kind of place where the doorman would have kicked my ass back to the street if I'd approached the front door in my Oregon Hill juvenile delinquency.

So that's where I took Cindy last night for the do-over for the dinner I reneged on the night before.

We talked about my straitened condition and its effects on our ability to pay the rent and buy groceries. Cindy's rather hefty alimony from Donnie Marshman, her real-estate mogul ex, is likely to end when she officially changes her mailing address to the Prestwould. On the upside, she owns the house where she's living. And soon she won't have any more college tuition and fees to pay. Plus, she—unlike almost every other alumna or alumnus in America—won't be wearing a five- or six-figure debt albatross around her neck on graduation day.

It was a crappy marriage, Cindy says, especially at the end, "but the cheating son of a bitch did send the checks on time."

Her big regret about the breakup is her son. Ronald Marshman Jr. is working for his father and sees a hell of a lot more of him than he does his mother. I haven't met young Chip, but I do question his ability to judge character.

In a strange confluence, he will be getting his degree from George Mason the week after Cindy and Andi graduate from VCU.

"We're going to be OK," Cindy assured me. "I can sell the house. And I'm going to get a job. Somebody's bound to need teachers."

Yes, I assure her, teachers are in great demand. Considering the language skills of the kids we get from various colleges as interns and part-timers, there is definitely a shortage of educators.

"But you don't really have to," I told her.

"I don't want to spend the rest of my life sitting on my butt watching the Food Channel," she said.

It isn't really the money that frosts my ass so much. Cindy's right. We'll get along somehow. Hell, if I wasn't so fond of the Prestwould, we could move into her place and save a four-figure rent check every month.

The thing I'm having a lot harder time swallowing than the free-range chicken breast I chowed down on last night is the realization that I really am just an item on the profit-loss ledger, something to be junked when some suit needs a new Jaguar, no matter how well I'm performing. I'll get it down, eventually, with enough bourbon and Zantac.

I told Cindy, truthfully and for the umpteenth time, that she is a good woman, and that I will find a way to make sure we don't wind up shopping for clothes at the thrift stores on Cary Street or buying past-sell-date bread.

I charged the bill for dinner on my VISA and hoped I had not made an empty promise to a woman who deserves better.

This morning, Sarah and I are out of town before Richmond's rush hour. I-64 beyond the airport is almost pleasant.

Cindy gave me grief about taking Sarah along, although she seems to be at least half kidding about my "robbing the cradle." She doesn't know that there is a bit of physical history between the lovely Ms. Goodnight and me. Knowledge, the Faber College motto notwithstanding, is not always good.

I see a strange car in Sarah's drive. Under duress, she confesses that she is "seeing" someone. When she assures me that the car does not belong to Mark Baer, with whom she had a short and regrettable relationship, I compliment her on her good taste.

"You haven't even met Tom," she says, sipping on her coffee.

"If he's not Baer, you've made a step up."

"Roger that."

Rita Dominick doesn't seem to be grooming Sarah for management these days. Sarah's stock sunk a little with the publisher, I think, when my young colleague opted not to enroll in MBA courses at the University of Richmond, a sure path to a publisher's office somewhere. That didn't displease me. I hate to see the best and the brightest sell out, even if it means we wind up being bossed by the mediocre.

Still she needs to do something. The idea of Sarah Goodnight going stale and cynical, gaining a couple of pounds a year and waking up one day wondering why the hell she went into print journalism, depresses me.

There is an opening for assistant metro editor, working for and with Sally Velez. I have encouraged Sarah to apply and told Sally she'd be a fool not to hire her if she does.

I prosecute my case further this morning. Print journalists these days, I tell Sarah, have to be like sharks. Keep moving or die. Either take a promotion or move to a bigger paper. Don't be like me. At fifty-six, you want to be the SOB, not the person who works for SOBs. You aren't likely to fire yourself.

"But you haven't done any of that."

"I rest my case."

"Maybe I don't want to be an SOB, or DOB, or whatever."

I tell her to see if she feels the same when they cut her hours or show her the door.

We leave it at that.

When we get to Chopper Ware's place, his truck is gone. I call him on his cell. He tells me he had an emergency of some kind at his hardware store, something about a leaky roof. I tell him we can go by the store. He says to wait until ten thirty.

So we go into Kilmarnock to kill time. We wind up back at the same diner where I found out who Biggio's insurance agent was. The same dyed-blonde waitress is working the tables.

"So," she says, "you down here to snoop around some more?"

I'm not sure if it's a good thing that she recognizes me, but she seems to not mind my "snooping."

She takes our orders. When she brings the coffee, she says, "Everybody down here's buzzing about that guy, that Biggio. I didn't know he was shackin' up with Marina Jacobs."

Shit. It didn't take long for Marina's cover to be blown. I didn't give her up, but I knew, deep down, that people would figure out who David Biggio's mystery honey was.

I told Sarah to order light. I want to take her to my favorite barbecue place on the way back to Richmond. I assure her that she will want to leave room in her flat little tummy for the J.C. Special at Pierce's.

We walk down the street, killing a little time in a used-book store. We get to Chopper Ware's hardware emporium about ten forty-five.

And he's gone. The clerk said he had to pick up some supplies. She didn't know when he would be back.

I mention to the clerk, who's between customers, that I wanted to catch up with Chopper and talk about old times, not mentioning that I'd never heard of or seen the man until last week.

"Well," the clerk says, "good luck getting Mr. Ware to talk about old times. He's not much on that kind of stuff."

"So he isn't from around here?"

She has to pause to wait on a paying customer.

"No," she says when she's free again. "I don't think he's related to any of the Wares around here. Didn't go to high school here, I know that."

She looks around, like somebody might be listening in.

"He kind of keeps it close to the vest, you know?"

She asks me what kind of guy 'ol Chopper was, me being a longtime buddy and all.

"We don't even know where he came from."

I tell her that maybe I'd better let Chopper himself answer that.

"He's always been the kind of guy that kept his own counsel," I tell her.

We kill some more time. Chopper Ware finally shows up shortly before one. He looks less than pleased that I've waited for him, although his countenance brightens and his manners improve when he sees Sarah has accompanied me.

"I don't have much time for you," he says, as he leads us back to his office. "Been busy as a one-eyed dog in a smokehouse."

I tell him that seems pretty busy, and we won't take up much of his time, now that we finally are in the same room with him.

He tells Sarah that she should keep better company and offers to take her on a little fishing expedition sometime.

Sarah tells him she doesn't fish.

"Well," Chopper says, "you drink, don't you?"

I look around the office. There are all kinds of plaques there noting that James "Chopper" Ware is in good standing with the Kiwanis, the Lions Club, the Chamber of Commerce, and just about anybody else who might have monthly meetings. There's a picture of him with one of our former governors. And there's one photograph of a teenage girl and a middle-aged woman. It's sitting on the shelf behind Chopper's desk.

Sarah and I let Chopper flirt for a while and tell a couple of off-color jokes. Finally I get down to business.

"Mr. Ware," I begin.

"Call me Chopper."

"Chopper, do you have any idea why David Biggio put your name on that insurance policy? I mean, it sounds like you didn't even know him all that well."

With the beard and gut, Chopper Ware could pass for Santa Claus if he ever chose to smile. He takes a sip of a Diet Coke. Too little, too late, I'm thinking.

"Hell, I don't know," he says. "I was as surprised as anybody when you told me. That damn Eddie Bonner, the insurance guy, he asked me that too."

I remark that normally you might put the name of a brother or sister, even if you hadn't seen them lately, or maybe your boss or somebody you worked with.

Chopper holds up his hands.

"Now I didn't say that I didn't know him at all. We did talk now and then, you know, with him living right there on the property. But he didn't tell me nothing about putting my name on some piece of paper."

He adds that some other "insurance guys" had been around. They were asking about Biggio's frame of mind.

"I told 'em his frame of mind looked fine to me. I think they're trying to figure a way to weasel out of paying his daughter. Bastards."

I take it a little further and ask Chopper who he thinks possibly would have called his former tenant three minutes before he crashed Chopper's plane. Who would even have known that he was up there, since the plane was stolen?

He spreads his arms out, almost knocking over the soft-drink can.

"Hell, who says they knew he was up there in my plane? It might have been a friend, if he had any, just calling to shoot the shit. Might of been somebody trying to sell him life insurance."

He laughs at his own joke.

I point out that the phone was made from one of those throwaways that people use when they don't necessarily want somebody to shine a light on their business.

"Well, hell. You know everything," Chopper says. "Why don't you tell me?"

If I knew everything, I tell him, I wouldn't be driving all the way down here on my day off to ask him questions.

"But there wasn't anybody else you know of out here who might've been close to him?"

He shakes his head.

"But I tell you, if I knew him all that well, I'd of known he was shacking up with that Jacobs woman."

I get around to asking Chopper about his life prior to Topping. Sarah checked the records. She confirmed that he bought the hardware store from the previous owner's family in 2000, and she found out that's when he bought the house overlooking the water.

"Not much to talk about before that," he says. "Not much I want to talk about. I think I told you that before."

He says it with a certain edge to his voice. And, when I press him on where he came from, he stands up and tells me we're done talking. He looks like he might be able to escort me out of the building whether I want to go or not, so we leave voluntarily.

Back on the street, I tell Sarah we have to make one more stop. This time she'll have to do the talking.

I park the car a block from Marina Jacobs's modest home. A drive-by told me her car was in the carport. I give Sarah as much background as I can on the woman whose life I've helped to make a little more difficult. I explain that I doubt that Willie Black would be welcome on the premises, but that a bright, young reporter such as herself, perhaps one who was thrown into the assignment blind after Mr. Black was demoted for unnamed offenses, might be able to get some information from Ms. Jacobs.

"Isn't that kind of deceptive?"

I explain that it certainly is. I further explain that the woman who slept with David Biggio at least once a week might be our best bet at finding out more than we know now.

"We won't use her name, or even refer to her as anything but 'a source,' but we need to talk to her."

"What if she refuses to talk to me, just because I happened to know you?"

"Tell her what an asshole I am, how I wouldn't even share my notes with you when I found out you were coming out here."

Sarah says she'll do it. I tell her we're doing this for the greater good. It's what I often tell myself when I'm poking my nose into other people's lives.

She comes back an hour later, just as I was about to go looking for her.

She gets in the car and pulls out her tape recorder.

"It took some doing," she says. "I haven't worked this hard at selling since I peddled Girl Scout cookies."

I express the opinion that the Thin Mints were an easier sale.

"You've got that right. She didn't want to talk to anybody who might even live in the same city as you. You've turned her against Richmond, Willie."

"So how did you get your foot in the door?"

Sarah says she had to convince her that Willie Black was a sneaky, untrustworthy bastard, three times divorced and prone to drunkenness and debauchery, and that he was close to getting fired from the newspaper. She told Ms. Jacobs that the paper sent her down to try to make this right.

"In other words, I just told the truth. It seemed to work."

I tell Sarah that she might have gone a little easier on the truth.

"Well," she says, "then you shouldn't have sent me in to clean up your mess. I did the best I could with what I had. And it worked."

Which, of course, is the bottom line.

Marina Jacobs didn't really have much else to say about her late lover. They weren't on the marriage track, she said, just "trying to make the night a little shorter, I guess."

Sarah gives me the CliffsNotes version. I can listen to the tape on the way back to town.

She asked Marina if she could remember anything out of the ordinary from the last Tuesday night she and David Biggio spent together, less than three days before he ended his life and a couple of dozen others.

Marina didn't remember anything at first. She said it was just like a couple of dozen other times. They'd been together about half a year, since they met at a café just outside Kilmarnock.

"But I did what you told me, Willie. Remember when I complained to you that I couldn't get people to tell me things? And you said to let the ears work. Just shut up and wait for it."

No, I don't remember telling her that. But I'll take credit, sage old mentor that I am.

"So we just sat there. I could hear the clock ticking. I was going to let a minute go past without saying anything.

"Then at about forty-five seconds—I was watching the second hand—she kind of perked up and said there was something, something she had forgotten, but now it came back to her.

"She said she woke up, and Biggio was already halfway out of bed, with his cell phone in his hand. She said the phone is probably what woke her up.

"She asked him if everything was OK, but he just waved her off and walked out the door into the living room."

He came back "maybe a minute or two later, she said." When Marina asked him who called, he said it was a wrong number. She told Sarah she didn't think anything much about it, just rolled over and went back to sleep.

"She said it seemed like a dream to her, but she knows it really happened."

OK, not much, but there's no reason for Marina Jacobs to make up something like that.

Sarah and I agree, as I wend my way from Route 3 to US 17 southbound, my taste buds already primed for a barbecue fix, that there isn't much we can do with this right now. It's just another brick in the wall I hope we're not building on shaky ground.

Thomas Jackson Bonesteel is murdered sometime the night of the fifth or early morning of the sixth. David Biggio gets a call while spending the night at Marina Jacobs's house, sometime after midnight. Less than three days later, Biggio does his deed.

SARAH DOES agree that I've led her to just about the best damn barbecue she's ever eaten. She orders a pound of Pierce's to go, even though I warn her that it's better eaten right on the premises. Still, I figure it would be a good idea to get a couple of sandwiches to take home to Cindy and Abe.

While trying to wipe some of the grease off her hands and mouth with paper napkins, she says she didn't really mean all the bad things she said about me to Marina Jacobs.

"I mean, I haven't seen you drunk for I'll bet a year at least. Wait, well, there was that one time at Chuck Apple's birthday party. But, I mean, you've had to slow down a little bit on the booze. I mean, no offense, but you're not getting any younger. And I'm sure you had very good reasons for all those divorces . . ."

I tell her to stop trying to make me feel better, because she sucks at it.

I drop Sarah off when we get back to Richmond, then head back to the Prestwould. I have nothing more to impart to our readers right now, so there's no reason to go by the paper, which is not paying me for today anyhow.

We still are allowed to turn in travel expenses, though, and I doubt that anyone in accounting will notice that I made a trip to Topping on my day off.

I'll ding them for breakfast and dinner. It's the least I can do. I'll even find a way to slip in that pound of 'cue Sarah brought home and the two sandwiches. Small victories are about all I can manage these days.

Back home, Custalow and Cindy are watching an old movie on TCM. Cindy kisses me and accuses me of being unfaithful to her.

"You went to Pierce's," she says. "I can smell it on your breath. You went to Pierce's without me."

I save the day by producing the greasy bag. One 'cue for her and one for Abe, with hush puppies.

"So," she says later, when we're curled up in bed, "did you find out anything today?"

I tell her that I did, but that one thing leads to another, and nothing I learned today led to a story for tomorrow's paper. The more answers I get, the more questions I have.

CHAPTER THIRTEEN

Wednesday

I was watching the Nats on TV last night when something I should have thought of a week ago passed through my pickled brain.

I smacked myself on the forehead. Cindy looked up from her book and said, "What? Is Strasburg getting shelled?"

So I told her about Pistol Pete Paquette.

Pistol Pete came here from Quincy, Massachusetts, in the early eighties. He started working for the paper the year before I did. Being almost equally young and stupid, we hung out together. I teased him for his "Bahstan" brogue and he got away with calling me "the man with the tan." We closed down a lot of bars. He had that funny speech thing some New Englanders have, where he sometimes sounded like Elmer Fudd. Like, he'd get "weally, weally wiled up" about something. People who weren't his friends were advised not to tease him much about that, though, because he was prone to "weally, weally" kick your ass if you "wubbed him wong."

Everyone called him "Pistol" because of an incident that, with a short amount of aging, evolved in the telling from near disaster to high comedy. Few at the paper are ancient enough to remember it now, and those who do have embellished it, the way we tend to do with the old-fart stories. I alone can tell it like it was, without gilding the lily (or, in this case, polishing the turd).

Pete and I shared night cops for a while. One of his nights, the police scanner alerted the newsroom to a hostage crisis over in Randolph, just on the other side of the Downtown Expressway.

Pete and a photographer went to the site. They cooled their heels for an hour or so while the police tried to sweet-talk the guy inside. He and his wife had had some kind of misunderstanding, and she had called the cops. Hubby took umbrage to that and was now holding her against her will. He was threatening to shoot her.

Then, sometime around midnight, the crew gathered outside (the TV folks were there too, of course, with cameras blazing) heard a single gunshot and then a scream.

The cops charged the front door. At the same time, a guy with a gun comes bursting out another door on the side of the house. It was, as luck would have it, the same side where Pete was hanging out, having a smoke. The guy was making a run for it, and his run took him within a few feet of Pete. Pete trips the gunman, who goes flying. When he looks up, he's looking in the face of a .38 Special—Pete's .38 Special.

When the cops get there, Pete Paquette is standing over the perp, who is lying on the ground begging him not to shoot.

Amazingly no one was injured. The idiot hostage-taker's gun had gone off accidentally, and he panicked and ran. The TV guys, to their delight, wound up with footage of our reporter standing over the guy with what turned out to be a loaded weapon.

"Fuck yeah, it was woaded," Pete told the cops. "Why the fuck would I be here with an empty gun?" Pete said "fuck" a lot. They got that on tape too.

The cops were kind of pissed. I guess they thought Pete was horning in on their territory. But they didn't charge him with anything. However, it was more than suggested by our paper's management at the time that Pete would no longer be packing heat when he went to crime scenes. He acceded, since he'd lose his job otherwise. After that, though, everybody from here to China knew him as Pistol Pete.

But Pete Paquette, wild and impetuous as he was, had some business sense. He saw that the guys who published papers lived in a hell of a lot better homes than the saps who worked for them. Pete's family had a little money, and between that and what some bank loaned him, he left us after about five years to take over a weekly.

The weekly was and is in the general vicinity of Topping. There's not a lot of crime to report in the area. The last time I saw Pete's paper, the front page was dominated by a story about a new secondhand clothing store moving into the old Wiener King building. Publishing's been good to Pistol Pete though. There's not much competition for ad dollars in that part of the state, and it turns out that a lot of folks like to read about what the school board did and who got a ticket for jaywalking. Hell, Pete's doing better with that weekly than we are with our fancy-pants big-city daily, I'm sure.

I haven't talked to him in a decade probably. I guess that's why I didn't connect him with David Biggio until last night.

Not wanting to make another trip down to the bay today, I'm choosing to pick my old friend's brain by telephone.

He answers the call himself. I notice that he has lost much of his accent over the years, or rather traded it in for one that makes him sound almost like he grew up with a view of the Chesapeake instead of Boston Harbor.

We laugh about the old stories, although I gather from Pete's tone that he'd just as soon not have his readers know about his pistol-packing past.

I am, of course, looking for information. The Biggio tragedy has given Pete and his staff of one reporter doubling as a photographer something other than the weather and the fishing report to put on the front page. What I'm really looking for, I tell him, is anything he can tell me about Chopper Ware.

"Chopper?" he says. "Oh, he's a character. One of my best advertisers. Can't say enough about him."

What I want to know, I tell Pete Paquette, is where did Ware come from?

"Hell, I don't know. A lot of the folks I deal with down here came from somewhere else. Like me. Mostly we don't get too nosy. You wouldn't last ten minutes."

Pete says he can look back in his files though.

"You said he came here in 2000? Yeah, that sounds about right. Let me check the clip files and see what I can come up with."

The weekly's files weren't on computer sixteen years ago, he tells me. He has to depend on the efficiency of some long-ago secretary to have clipped a particular story.

"We always do a piece when a new business opens," Pete says. "We'll have that one, unless old Myrtle was having a bad day."

It turns out "old Myrtle" was on her A game. Paquette calls me back within an hour and tells me he has found the story.

"Must be forty inches at least," he says. "You've got to understand, Willie, having a hardware store stay in town is a really big deal around here."

It almost sounds like he said "weally." I don't mention that.

I ask him if he remembers seeing Biggio around town, or anywhere else. He says he doesn't, that the guy didn't make much of an impression.

"We didn't even know about him and Marina Jacobs until that story came out and everybody started blabbing about it."

Pete or somebody in his employ is able to scan the story and send it to me as an attachment. There's a picture too, back when Chopper Ware's beard had not grown to Clausian size and the man himself was many stones lighter. It reproduces amazingly well.

I call Pete Paquette back and thank him for his generosity. We promise to get together soon and have a beer or three, both knowing it probably won't happen.

"How's it feel," he asks me before we hang up, "being back on night cops again?"

Not bad, I tell him, but there are days when I'd like to borrow that .38 of his.

Nothing much I've learned of late is going to push the ball forward, for now. So since Cindy doesn't have any morning classes, we decide to go for a walk over to Belle Isle, which will take us through Oregon Hill and by Peggy's, so I can check in on my mother, daughter, and grandson.

It's a great day to be outside in Richmond, the kind of honeysuckle-scented wonder that makes you temporarily forget it'll probably be forty-five degrees and raining tomorrow. We find Peggy sitting out front, conversing with Jerry Cannady, her next-door neighbor, while William, two months shy of his second birthday, is still less than steady on his feet and seems very capable of doing a high-dive off the porch. My mother, either stoned or more confident of William's motor skills than I am, seems unperturbed. I've asked Andi, who's in class now, if she really trusts her dear old granny with a twenty-two-month-old. She offered to let me keep him instead.

Cannady's being civil today, so I do my best to return the favor. He is often a meddlesome asshole, somewhere around a nine on the Feldman scale, but even he can't be but so snippy on a day like this.

Awesome Dude is nowhere to be seen. This is the kind of weather that makes my mother's itinerant long-term guest yield to the call of the wild, knowing that he is free to yield to the equally seductive call of the tame come dinnertime.

I look forward to taking my grandson on walks down to the river in the near future, maybe three months from now if he doesn't break his neck stumbling off the porch under my mother's watchless eye. I see trips on the horizon to watch the Flying Squirrels play baseball. I fear that taking him down to Belle Isle today, though, would end with either Cindy or me carrying him back, a mile or so uphill.

So we strike out toward the James, leaving William to perfect his perambulating.

I tell Cindy about my so-far unsuccessful efforts to learn more about David Biggio's landlord. Nobody else seems all that interested in the fact that he kind of showed up out of nowhere, in the middle of nowhere, sixteen years ago. Nobody else seems to think it strange that he is the person Biggio chose to put down as a contact when he took out that big-ass life-insurance policy. Or that it was his plane Biggio used as his murder-suicide weapon.

"Well," Cindy says, "I mean, he was living on this guy's property, and the guy did have a plane. If he was going to steal one, that'd probably be the one.

"As for Ware," Cindy says, "sometimes people just want to start over."

She tells me about a man who came to work for her ex-husband. He was a crackerjack real-estate salesman. The man could sell fleas to a dog.

"He just kind of appeared out of nowhere, but he could move houses. He did a great job. I think he was salesman of the year one year."

She stops.

"Oh, yeah. Oops. Maybe not such a good analogy."

"What?"

"I forgot. About five years after he came to work for Donnie, the cops came looking for him. As it turned out, he had a wife and kids that he'd walked out on. He had made himself disappear. By the time they caught up with him, he'd married again and started another family."

I tell her, in the name of full disclosure, that I am going to pass around the photograph I have of Chopper Ware from sixteen years ago, and that one of the people I'll be passing it around to is Kate Ellis. My ex has connections that I don't have. Between her, Marcus Green, and what's left of Bartley, Bowman and Bush, maybe somebody will remember that face.

It's just a hunch. I mean, Ware could have come from anywhere, from Walla Walla to Tallahassee. There's something, though, in his accent, that makes me think he lived much closer to Topping than those places in his former life. I have an ear for accents. I could be in Timbuktu, and if a tour bus full of West End Richmonders came rolling up, I've have them ID'd before they got off the bus. I hear something familiar in Chopper Ware's speech, something he's tried to get rid of but can't quite shake.

Ware's probably just a harmless old curmudgeon who wants to be left alone for no other reason than he wants to be left alone, I admit to Cindy.

People who try to hide, though, pique my interest.

She says she's OK with my running it past Kate "as long as you keep both feet on the floor." I promise to remain upright.

We spend a pleasant couple of hours walking down and back to the pedestrian walkway and over to the island. On the return trip, nobody's outside at my mother's house. There's no evidence that the rescue squad has been there, and William's body isn't lying in the yard, so I guess everything's OK.

"Do you think your mom's able to look after him?" Cindy asks. "I mean, she seems kind of, um, lackadaisical."

I point out that that was the way she raised me, and look how well I turned out.

"Are you sure," she asks, "that you didn't fall on your head a time or two?"

THERE IS time, before punching in, to check in with the Klassens.

Things are not going well, insurance-wise. Louisa is home alone. Bobby's back at work, and Brandy's in school.

The former Louisa Biggio lets me in. She has circles under her eyes and what looks suspiciously like a bruise on her arm.

"Bobby got a little drunk last night," she says. "He's real upset about the way it's going."

The insurance bloodhounds have been around, it seems. They have come to the conclusion that Biggio did exactly what he intended to do when he crashed Chopper Ware's plane into Dark Star.

"They said that the FAA, or whoever it was, couldn't find any reason to suspect engine failure or anything like that, so they say they're going with suicide unless something else shows up.

"Bobby said he was going to sue their asses, and one of the guys, he just laughed and said go right ahead."

They've contacted Marcus Green, and she says Marcus is looking into it. If I know Marcus, he won't do much looking unless there's a payday at the end of the rainbow. Maybe Kate can do the Klassens some good, when and if she comes back to work at Green and Ellis.

About the only lame-ass advice I can give her is to "hang in there." There's nothing I can truthfully tell her from my snooping around in Topping and Kilmarnock that will ease her mind. Louisa Klassen and her daughter have gotten a raw deal. Her asshole second husband, who probably has never had two nickels to rub together, was no doubt projecting. He'd already plowed through the half-million, in that pea brain of his, and now he feels like he's been robbed. He's the kind of guy who could win the lottery and be bankrupt in two years.

I tell Louisa to keep the faith, and that I'll call her when I learn anything useful.

I drive by the site of the crash. It is likely to be a gaping, ugly hole in the former Devil's Triangle for some time to come. The 7-Eleven is about the only thing that's still open. I see three guys sitting on the curb, maybe including Cottonmouth, my reliable source.

A car is parked on the street next to the store, facing the scene of the crime. I recognize the occupant and realize I won't have to go by Kate's house after all.

I park behind her. She sees me in the side-view mirror as I walk up and unlocks the passenger door.

I suggest that she probably could find a better place to regain her mental stability.

"I know," she says. "I can't stay away though. I can't figure out why this happened. Why would anybody do something like this, Willie?"

Nobody can figure that one out, I tell her, not until we know more than we do now. But why come here?

She says because it's the last place Greg was alive.

"Plus I can't stay around that house. It smells like him. I can't open a shirt drawer without being damn near brought to my knees. I never thought I had that keen a sense of smell, but now the whole house smells like Greg. I had to get away. This was as good a place as any."

A neighbor is keeping Grace, and Kate has to be back in an hour.

I bring out the file I planned to drop by her house.

"It's just a shot in the dark," I tell her, "but this is an old picture of the guy whose plane Biggio used. I think he might be from around here. I'm handing copies of the story in the weekly down there, plus a picture of him, the way he looked sixteen years ago, to people who know Richmond. See if anybody at BB&B recognizes him."

She says she will pass the information on to the older partner who didn't go to happy hour with the rest that night. She tells me the guy has had no luck linking David Biggio to the firm. Neither he nor anybody he's talked with from the old days remembers anything about Biggio, and he doesn't show up in any of the company's files, going back to the 1980s.

"I don't know, Willie. It just seems like a random nutcase."

She shakes her head. A tear is trickling down her right cheek. I catch it with my index finger, for some damn reason.

"I can't decide," she says, "whether I'd be more upset if I found out the bastard just shut his eyes and brought that plane down wherever it crashed, willy-nilly, or if I found out he hit the exact target he wanted to hit."

There are no good answers, I concede, at least none that are going to make sleep come any easier anytime soon.

I kiss her on the cheek. I can taste the salt from that one tear.

She smiles at me and thanks me. It makes me think that, possibly, we can be friends. That would not suck.

One thing about being cut to thirty hours a week: The publisher doesn't have the gall to ride me quite as hard. Wheelie isn't breathing down my neck as her proxy, wanting the next big thing on David Biggio. That ought to be good, but it's not. There is this feeling that I've taken the cutoff marked "Oblivion 5 miles." I'm the old coot who got his hours cut but, hey, he's got one foot out the door anyhow, right? Next stop: retirement party.

I think everybody else here is more than happy, at this point, to wait for the police to call the Dark Star tragedy either a one-man murder-suicide or an unfortunate accident caused by a crazy man who decided to steal an airplane. We'll do a big commemorative piece a year from now, and Dark Star will go from being a news story to being an unpleasant bit of local lore.

There's more emphasis now on the Jack Bonesteel mess. Nobody can figure out which of Bonesteel's many enemies might have used him for target practice. The fact that Candidate Number One, David Biggio, apparently was in bed with his lady friend seventy-some miles away at the time of the murder muddies the water considerably.

At any rate, I'm letting Baer run with the Bonesteel story. He's in his element, filing A1 stories daily and blogging diarrhetically. It's all conjecture and bullshit, of course. L.D. Jones apparently is more willing to talk with Baer than he is to me. Hell, he'd rather talk to a telemarketer than me. But what he's feeding Baer isn't actually leading anywhere, because the chief doesn't have a clue. But it's fun to make guesses and put out theories. Who knows? One of them might be right.

Baer comes around to see if he can pump me for information. He knows I've been down to Topping a couple of times.

I tell him that he knows what I know. There is no reason at this time to share any of my hunches or suspicions with a guy who seems to like putting hunches and suspicions in the newspaper. If I find out anything germane, I tell him, he'll be the first to know. "By reading it in the paper like everyone else" is the part I leave unsaid.

My night passes quietly, beating the odds. Usually the first fine spring days seem to set the table for mayhem. The sap rises, and the saps start shooting each other.

Tonight there's nothing worse than a couple of domestics resulting in flesh wounds.

Plenty of time to work on my solitaire, wander over to Penny Lane for a couple of beers while Sally covers for me, and wonder if I'm barking up a tree that's not even in the right forest.

CHAPTER FOURTEEN

Thursday

Custalow's breaking in a new maintenance guy at the Prestwould today to replace the one Feldman managed to get fired. It speaks to McGrumpy's popularity around here that the residents took up a collection for the poor soul who got canned. They came up with almost $2,000. I was good for ten bucks, big spender that I am.

"Maybe you ought to spread the word around here that your hours have been cut," Cindy suggested. "You know, go for the sympathy vote. You could see how beloved you are by your neighbors."

I tell her I would, but I'm afraid of what I might find out.

"Plus, some of them are kind of giving me the fish-eye already, what with me living in sin and all."

This, of course, is bullshit. A startling number of the septuagenarian (and beyond) residents here are either cohabitating or doing what we call the elevator ride of shame after sleepovers with their neighbors. We are a tolerant group here, Feldman notwithstanding.

"Honey," one widow in the other tower told me at the Christmas party, "we're old. We ain't dead."

Cindy says she'll move out if it'll ease my shame. I decline.

There are some places I want to go before my workday officially begins. When I tell Cindy about wanting to pass Chopper Ware's picture around to some of my more ubiquitous friends, she points out that she probably can save me some shoe leather.

She takes a photo of Ware's image from the year 2000 with her iPhone, e-mails it to me and then tells me to feel free to forward.

I would have thought of that, I tell her.

"Of course you would have," she says with something very close to a smirk.

So I put the word out. Basically, has anybody ever seen this guy before? It's a long shot, but like the lottery folks say, if you don't play, you'll never win.

I check our paper's website to see if anything newsworthy happened overnight. Usually this is a waste of time. Today, though, is the exception. Our web jockeys have put up a story that catches my eye right away. Unfortunately it's not our story. It's from the *Washington Post*, and it's about the late Thomas Jackson Bonesteel.

I figured we'd seen the last of the *Post* for a while, but I was wrong. Their one-person bureau has stopped sniffing around the Dark Star story, assuming all the meat's been picked from those bones.

What their guy did, though, was do a piece on Bonesteel. It's what big papers do. They swoop into some smaller paper's backyard and scarf up everything that's been written about a big local story. Then they more or less rewrite it and present it to their readers as fresh copy. They make an occasional bow to the "local paper," but mostly they just poach. For a story in Richmond, they tend to, as Sally Velez puts it, usually with clenched teeth, "put the Mayberry on it." You can count on a big takeout from these parts having some reference to "the folks in Richmond." You expect a quote from Cousin Goober.

Hell, I can only bitch so much. We've done the same thing. Big story in Lynchburg or Danville comes to our attention, we've been known to come wheeling in a week later and rewrite our way to a state press association award.

One thing made this one worth noting though. There actually was more detail than we'd been able to glean. Somebody in the police department, no doubt with L.D. Jones's blessing, told the *Post* guy something that Gillespie either withheld or didn't know about and Baer hasn't been able to dig up.

Bonesteel's body, according to the *Post* story, had been marked by his killer. Someone had taken a knife and done a little artwork on his chest. The late lawyer had the letters SAP cut into him. According to the *Post*, the guy seemed to have been dead when the whittling began. Small favors.

The cops, again according to the *Post*, didn't have much to go on. Nobody saw anyone strange in the neighborhood, and no one remembered any unusual cars.

All this, of course, will make Baer look like an asshole—which he is. But still I ache for him. He's still drawing a full paycheck, and as such, he can expect to incur the full wrath of Rita Dominick. Already beaten by the *Post*, he can expect a second flogging as soon as the publisher is able to get him within yelling distance.

I call Peachy Love at home and am lucky enough to catch her before she heads in to work.

"Aw, you know, Willie," she says. "The chief loves attention. The *Post* guy made him feel like he was big-time, I guess. Plus no affection on his part for any place where you work, no offense."

So L.D. fed that choice morsel to the *Post* and left us twisting in the wind. I want to call him and chew his ear personally, but that would only give the bastard satisfaction. Plus he'd probably call Dominick and complain. She'd take his side.

I'VE AGREED to meet Andi for lunch. She wants me to start bonding with her new boyfriend. She's been bartending at a place in Scott's Addition and swears that they have killer sandwiches, so that's where we go.

There are all these new joints that I haven't tried out. What could be better than Spaghetti Albert, after all? Some of them are good, I'm sure, but they seem to be trying too damn hard. There's a place called Lunch where you can have breakfast, right next to a place called Supper, where you can have lunch. My head hurts.

Once we've been introduced and are seated, Andi's new love interest seems a little nervous. I have to admit, I'm not making it any easier on him. Maybe I'm a little, um, terse. At one point, I am terse enough that Andi kicks me under the table.

Hey, I've got my reasons. I already know that Peggy has taken care of young William overnight on more than one occasion so my daughter could trip the light fantastic with this guy. One child out of wedlock is youthful indiscretion. Two, by two different men, would start to sound like a trend.

Mainly I'm playing the odds. Andi's choice of men has been shitty so far. Why should this jerk be any different?

He doesn't seem cut from the same cloth as Thomas Jefferson Blandford V, father of my grandson, though. I'll give him that. As a matter of fact, he doesn't appear to have the same fatal combination of laziness and arrogance that has marked so many of my daughter's previous flames. Is it any wonder that 60 percent of the kids getting into college are female?

His name is Walter, not Walt or Wally. He seems like a bit of a nerd. He wears glasses and looks like he weighs about 150. He is looking for something vegetarian on a decidedly carnivore menu. He's already graduated, but he's a couple of years younger than Andi, who has casually strolled through academia while Walter seems to have been sprinting. He's doing graduate work, on track to be a physician's assistant which, I am told by Andi, is a rather remunerative way to earn a living, to say nothing of secure. People might stop reading the newspaper, but they aren't damn likely to stop getting sick.

Walter, whose last name is McGinness, seems to think I have the most fascinating job in the world, unless he's blowing smoke up my ass. Either way I appreciate the effort. Bonus points for Walter: Andi says he's crazy about my grandson.

All in all, it goes well. Many of Andi's beaus have been of such poor quality that my daughter hasn't dared introduce us. I do not exchange Christmas cards with the ones I have gotten to know. Walter does seem a cut above, even if that makes him a tall midget.

A world-class club sandwich, a couple of Millers, and an unexpectedly pleasant lunch with Andi and her latest have me feeling a little mellow.

THE NEWSROOM succeeds in harshing my mellow in no time flat.

I check in about five minutes after three. Stepping off the elevator, I wonder if we've had a bomb threat, because I don't see a damn soul.

And then I hear Rita Dominick's voice at the other end of the room, over by Sports. Staff meeting. They never have these anymore to impart good news. I consider retracing my steps, but what you don't know can actually hurt you.

The forty or so staffers present are gathered in a circle around Bootie Carmichael's desk, listening to our publisher ream us a new one.

I slip into the group, standing beside Sarah. She looks at me and shakes her head.

". . . and I want to know," Dominick is saying, "why we keep getting scooped on stories by a competitor that has one reporter, one reporter in this town. Can anybody tell me that?"

I'm thinking, Jesus Christ, lighten up.

Baer is standing near her. He looks like he might cry.

"This is the second time in the last few days we've been beaten on a major story here by the *Post*," she says. Looking around, she spots me and nods in my direction, more or less including me in the same general species of worthless incompetent as Baer.

It is astounding to me that a woman who just recently got locally famous for accidentally flushing her cell phone down a toilet can have the gall to stand up and hector anybody about anything. For not the first time, I am struck with what a goddamn great thing it is to have no shame.

She goes on about how we have to be the Number One, go-to source for news in our city, like we aren't about 99 percent of the time.

I'm thinking: You couldn't have just called Baer to your office and chewed on his ass in private?

Somebody should stop her and tell her nobody even remembers anymore who first told a breathless world that David Biggio left his daughter with a half-million-dollar life-insurance policy she'll probably never see. Nobody will give a shit in two days about who first told our readers that somebody was playing tic-tac-toe on Thomas Jackson Bonesteel's body. Somebody should, but nobody in this room is that crazy about unemployment, myself included.

Bootie is sitting just behind her, so he has the luxury of not having to appear riveted by the boss's little lecture. When he rolls his eyes, it causes one of the features editors to snort, which causes Dominick to turn her head. Bootie looks innocent as a cherub, which almost cracks me up.

"If you people think this is funny, I guarantee you won't think it's funny much longer," she says. She leaves that hanging like a malevolent fart and starts to stride back to her den.

One of the sports interns breaks the silence.

"Ms. Dominick?" he calls.

She almost doesn't turn around, but then she does.

He holds up an object in his right hand.

"You forgot your cell phone."

Some of the staffers are able to stifle themselves. Looking around, I see others' mouths twitching. Dominick snatches the phone from the kid, who looks somewhat stricken. She storms out, and most of us don't actually break down until she's safely on the elevator.

Ray Long, who is as old as I am, is actually sitting on the floor, he's laughing so hard. There isn't a dry eye in the house.

Rita Dominick has inadvertently given our hard-ridden staff something to laugh about on an otherwise cheerless day.

A couple of reporters commiserate with Baer, who normally neither deserves nor receives sympathy. Even I, hardly the Number One member of his fan club, stop by and reassure him that the sun does not shine on the same dog's ass every day and that even a blind hog will find an acorn once in a while. Baer looks puzzled.

"Where do you get that crap?" Sarah asks me as we're walking back toward our desks. "Did people actually once talk like that?"

"You should be taking notes," I tell her. "I won't always be around to educate you."

"What do you think she meant by 'much longer'?" Sally Velez asks me.

I tell her it beats me. If she means we're about to be sold, then lead me to the auction block. Check my teeth and send me down South. Anything would be better than this crap.

Of course, that's what I might have said about our last publisher, the one I'm kind of nostalgic for right now.

Cheer up, I tell Sally. Things can always get worse.

She says that's what she's afraid of.

Nothing else manages to match the drama of our publisher's little shit fit for the next few hours.

Then about eight thirty, I get a call.

I welcome the distraction. It takes me away from rewriting a police handout Peachy sent us on the latest police initiative to "reach out" to our community. If we nurture the Future Criminals of America, maybe they won't kill each other or us when they come of age. So the enlightened reasoning goes. It's a noble idea, but I know cops who swear they deal with people all the time who were born evil and will die evil. It's a hard theory to debunk when you've seen what some of these guys have seen. It's hard for me to dismiss it. Kids I grew up with in Oregon Hill, a couple of them were mean as snakes when they were four, they were mean as snakes at fourteen, and they're as mean as ever now at fifty-four or whatever.

At any rate, any call would have been welcome. This one, though, is a blessing.

"Willie?" Kate says. "I think we might know who he is."

SHE'S THE first of my far-flung sources to respond to the copy of Chopper Ware's sixteen-year-old photograph.

She did pass it along to the oldest surviving partner of BB&B, Fred Byron. She left it on his desk with a note. He called her back a few hours ago.

He said he couldn't be positive, but that the man I know as Chopper Ware bore a remarkable resemblance, in that 2000 photo, to a man named James Patton.

"He said he remembered the face because of all the hell the guy raised with the firm."

I ask for enlightenment.

"You might remember it. It was back in 1997, Byron said. Patton was a store manager or something at one of the local groceries. His daughter was killed by a hit-and-run driver. BB&B defended the kid who hit her."

It's ringing a vague bell.

Apparently the folks at Kate's old firm did a good job, because she says the partner who recognized Chopper Ware as James Patton remembers the accused got off with a very light sentence.

"The father more or less went batshit in court when they handed down the sentence. He had to be ushered out of the courtroom. Mr. Byron says he'd never seen anyone angrier."

The old BB&B partner was a little vague on the details. I thank Kate and tell her I probably can take it from here. She sounds better. Maybe she's dragging herself back into the world.

I ask her if Marcus is showing any interest in taking young Brandy Klassen's case. She says she doesn't know. She still hasn't returned to the offices of Green and Ellis.

"I talked to him about it, though, and he said it didn't look too winnable."

I have time to check our files, which mercifully have been electronic since well before 1997.

I was covering the legislature at the time, so I had nothing to do with the case. As I caught up on my reading, though, it came back to me.

James Patton was a produce manager at Ukrop's. He was forty-three years old when his life changed in a horrible and irreversible way.

Sometime after one A.M. one April night, his daughter, Susanna Alford Patton, was coming home from a party when she apparently had car trouble. Something, anyhow, made her get out of the car on a particularly shoulderless part of River Road, over past the University of Richmond.

She was struck by a hit-and-run driver. They caught the bastard, two days later, when he tried to get a Maaco paint job to cover up the damage.

It turned out that the driver was a college student, the twenty-two-year-old son of a man who had enough money to buy really good lawyers. He might have gone to Marcus Green if Marcus had been up and running at the time, although the father was the kind of old money Richmonder who probably would have gravitated toward the sort of lawyers who lived in his neighborhood and were of a paler hue than Marcus.

So he went to Bartley, Bowman and Bush. They served him well.

Witnesses at a fraternity party that night testified that the driver seemed to be on the far side of drunk when he left about twelve thirty. He managed to hit another student's car on the way out of the parking lot.

I guess the BB&B boys figured their best bet was to blame the victim. Reading the stories, I can see that they did everything they could to suggest that Susanna Patton was a wild girl, out partying herself and putting herself drunkenly into harm's way on that deadly stretch of River Road. They brought in people from the party she attended who said she might have had one or two drinks. One young man, whose father, it turned out later, worked as an accountant for the father of the accused, said he was "sure" she was inebriated.

The stories mention that James and Dorothy Patton attended every session of the trial. Susanna was their only daughter.

They even managed to bring up the dead girl's sexual history, such as it was. The same boy who said she was drunk said she had a reputation for being a little loose, a little round of heel.

It was dirty pool, the kind of crap where the well-groomed and well-mannered hire goons to make sure that justice doesn't get in the way of the family legacy.

By the time the lawyers were through, they had managed to frame a story about two drunken partiers, one of whom accidentally killed the other one, and then panicked and fled. Could have happened to anyone.

Despite the fact that forensic evidence showed that Susanna Patton almost certainly was off the road when she was hit and killed, BB&B's best were able to plant enough doubt that the prosecutor wound up offering a plea. James Patton was quoted as saying the prosecutor had sold out, that his daughter deserved better.

I'm sure she did, but she didn't get it. Instead, two months after the trial, a judge sentenced the driver to ten years, all suspended, and took away his driver's license.

The same day they sentenced him, there was a story about a drug dealer on the other side of town who got twenty-five years.

Doing a further search for James Patton, I found he appears in our paper on three subsequent occasions.

On a November day in 1999, two and a half years after her daughter's death, Dotty Patton took an overdose of sleeping pills and died before anyone found her. She and James Patton had been separated for five months when it happened.

Three months later, the house belonging to James and Dorothy Patton was listed as sold.

And about a year later, James Patton settled out of court with the family whose son had killed his daughter. The amount wasn't released, but Patton was quoted as saying that he was going to use the money to start over "if I can."

That was the last hit I got for James Patton.

There was one picture of James and Dotty Patton leaving the courtroom after the first day of the trial. Looking at it and trying to imagine James Patton eighty pounds heavier and with a long white beard, I am fairly certain I have already met him.

We ran a mug shot of Susanna Patton several times during the trial and after the sentencing. Looking at it, I am pretty damn sure I have seen her face before, enclosed in a frame in Chopper Ware's office.

As I'm finishing my stroll through the archives, something occurs to me. I check the exact date of Susanna Patton's hit-and-run death.

April 8.

CHAPTER FIFTEEN

Friday

It's my own damn fault. I sent Jumpin' Jimmy Deacon a copy of Chopper Ware's 2000 photo, because he seems to know everyone in Richmond.

"Yeah," he says when I answer the phone just before sunrise, "that fella you asked about. Jumpin' Jimmy knew him. He used to work at Ukrop's. Patton. Jimmy Patton. I remember because it was just like my name, and Patton was my favorite general."

I thank Jimmy for confirming what the BB&B partner told Kate. I don't suggest that he might call at a more civil hour. You take your sources, warts and all.

My brain is a little fried. We did shut down Penny Lane last night, it being almost the weekend. Cindy came down and joined us. She enjoyed the myriad recountings of Rita Dominick's amusing adventures with cell phones.

Now that I'm awake, though, my brain won't let me get back to sleep. The revelation that Chopper Ware almost certainly used to go by another name, and that in his previous incarnation he had every reason in the world to despise Bartley,

Bowman and Bush, has my imagination bouncing around like a pinball machine on crack.

I want to write something about all this, but where's the hook? I can't even swear that Chopper Ware and James Patton are the same person. And if so, what of it? Chopper Ware wasn't flying his plane when it obliterated Dark Star.

It's time to write what I know, though, and let people draw their own conclusions. Hell, I don't even know what my own conclusions are. The trick will be writing something that can get past Wheelie, the publisher, and our lawyers.

A morning spent knocking on doors in James Patton's old North Side neighborhood doesn't yield much. Of the five people who answered, only two lived there sixteen years ago, and neither of them has seen or heard of Patton since he left. His wife had been living in the house from the separation until her death, and then Patton moved back, they told me.

He had become, the two neighbors concurred, a little strange by then. And when I showed them the 2000 photo of James "Chopper" Ware from the Northern Neck paper, they agreed that it was either Patton or his identical twin.

It is essential that I at least give Ware a chance to rebut the claims that he lived another life with another name in Richmond before his appearance in Topping.

I call his house and leave a message. The message is that I want to ask him a few questions about a man named James Patton.

What if Chopper calls back and says he has no idea what I'm talking about? For that matter, what if he says that he's entitled to change his name and start over if he wants to? This one won't exactly be what you'd call hard news. It will be the kind of story that leaves more questions than answers. I'll just lay it out there. One: Chopper Ware bears a remarkable resemblance to a man who disappeared from the Richmond area about the same time Ware bought a store and a house out near the bay. Two: The man who so greatly resembles Chopper, James Patton, bore a ginormous grudge against the law firm of Bartley, Bowman and Bush. Three: The guy who crashed into Dark Star and took out much of BB&B's best and brightest, along with a slew of innocent civilians, was flying a plane stolen from Chopper Ware.

Seems like a story to me. When I run it by Wheelie, though, he's a little less impressed than I am.

"We can't prove any of this."

"We can put a picture of James Patton next to one of Chopper Ware, back before he grew the world's biggest beard. We can let the readers connect the dots."

Wheelie shakes his head.

"Have we even talked to this guy Ware yet?"

I tell him that I have a call in.

"Well," Wheelie says, hoping to avoid a potential lawsuit or at least put it off a bit, "wait and see what he says."

I promise to do that, although I'm pretty sure what Chopper's going to say.

I check with Peachy at police headquarters. She shouldn't do this, but she lets me swear her to secrecy. After she takes the oath, I ask her if there are any outstanding warrants on a guy named James Patton. She checks and says there aren't any.

I also do a check on the rich man's son who ended Susanna Patton's life much too early. After searching our files and then Googling him, I determine that he is now a successful businessman living outside Chicago. Apparently his youthful indiscretion did not greatly cloud his future.

In the meantime, I write what I can write and wait for Chopper Ware to confirm or deny. It's still only noon. Maybe Chopper will check his voice mail over lunch.

I also weigh in with Mark Baer, who looks like he's been working harder than ever, trying to get back into our publisher's good graces and avoid getting "scooped" by the *Washington Post* again.

He hasn't found out anything else worth writing about. He's also had his eyes opened as to how far he can trust L.D. Jones.

I could have told him that, but he probably wouldn't have listened.

"Nobody saw anything," he says. "I walked up and down that street. Somebody even called the cops on me. I don't think they're used to reporters wandering through their boxwoods."

"And nobody's got a clue about the letters?"

Baer shakes his head.

"Nothing that the damn cops will share with me."

"Ongoing investigation."

"Right."

I tell him to hang in there. I hint, without giving Baer any real information, that something might be developing.

"Just a hunch," I tell him.

Sally, Chuck Apple, and I go to lunch at Perly's. I bounce what I have already off both of them. They are in agreement with Wheelie that I have to get some kind of statement from Chopper Ware, even if the statement is along the lines of "fuck you."

And when we get back to the newsroom, all hell has broken loose.

The news has been sent to the staff via e-mail. We are being sold.

The buyer owns a chain of newspapers, mostly in the Southeast. I've heard of them, and most of what I've heard isn't all that great. Is it possible that things really could get worse?

MediaWorld's world is mostly bounded by the Potomac on the north and the Mississippi on the west. We will be the largest paper in its little empire. It is to the credit of our corporate masters' ability to keep a secret that we proud newshounds had not even heard a rumor about MediaWorld.

They are buying us for a ridiculously small amount of money, reflecting newspapers' relevance and value to twenty-first-century society. If the whole paper only brings that much, Enos Jackson wonders, how much can each of us peons be worth? Like our soon-to-be-former chain's stock, we're talking pennies on the dollar.

Our publisher comes through an hour or so after the bombshell hits. Rita Dominick seems sanguine about the whole thing, as she should be. The chain that sold us to MediaWorld will no doubt be packing her off to some other exotic locale soon, maybe a TV station this time, or even corporate headquarters, where accountability is something to be suffered only by the little people.

Well at least we soon will have a different headache. We could use some variety.

"Nothing will change here," Dominick says. "Things will be just the same."

She says it like a threat.

"And I'll be staying on for a few months to help with the transition."

If that's supposed to be good news, nobody claps.

A couple of people ask about our pensions. We are assured that they are safe. That money will remain in the capable hands of the company that just sold us for forty pieces of silver.

Handley Pace in design asks if we'll be reducing staff.

"Not in the near future," our publisher says.

We trust our former owners as far as we can throw them. We're just going to have to hold our breaths about those pensions.

And when the brass says there absolutely, positively will not be any more staff reduction, it means "maybe." When the brass says "not in the near future," it's jump time for those of us young enough to land on our feet.

For Sally, me, and about half the crowd wandering around the newsroom semi-dazed right now, the time to leap has long passed. All we can do is ride this baby down and hope somebody finds a way to restart the engine.

IN BETWEEN a couple of shootings, one fatal and one not, I have time to do a little digging.

With Sarah's help, I find out that James Patton left almost no family behind. With his wife and only child dead and his parents already deceased, the closest thing we could find to a relative was a half-brother. And, son of a bitch, the half-brother died of cancer last year.

James Patton, whoever he was or is, had little reason to stick around Richmond, it seems.

I have almost given up hope of hearing from Chopper Ware when the phone rings at eight fifteen.

"You left me a message," he says, or rather growls. "Something about some fella I never heard of."

I tell him what I'm pretty sure he already knows.

He's silent for what seems like a long time.

"If you write any of this bullshit," he says, "I'll sue your goddamn pants off."

I ask him flat-out.

"Are you James Patton?"

"I am James Ware. James Fucking Ware."

I ask him where James Fucking Ware was before the year 2000.

"What right do you have to snoop around in my life? What business is it of yours where or who I was before I came out here? I'm an honest businessman, just trying to make a living. Isn't it enough that the son of a bitch destroyed my plane?"

True enough, maybe, about the snooping, if I wasn't being paid to pull a news story out of my butt every once in a while.

I ask him where he was at five thirty P.M. on the eighth, as his plane was plowing into Dark Star. It's a fairly straightforward question.

"Why do you want to know that?"

I tell him that I want to know because the cops are eventually going to want to know, and I thought I might beat them to the punch.

"If it's any of your goddamn business, I was out fishing. Gone all afternoon. Didn't get back in until seven or so."

"By yourself?"

"Yes, by my damn self. But I'm sure somebody would have seen me, and a whole bar full of people saw me that night. Now you've wasted about as much of my time as you're going to."

I try to explain that we have a couple of people here in town who are pretty sure he and James Patton are one and the same, and that the photo I saw on his desk in Kilmarnock is—I stop myself from saying "a dead ringer"—almost identical to one I saw of Susanna Patton that ran in our paper after her death.

"You leave her out of it," he says. "I swear to God, if you run this crap in that ass-wipe paper of yours, you will rue the day you were born."

So, I ask him, is that a "yes" or a "no" on the Patton-Ware question?

He hangs up.

I come around to Sally's desk and tell her where we stand.

"Jesus, Willie," she says. "The guy didn't even confirm or deny it."

"I take it more like: he didn't deny it."

"He also didn't deny that he'd sue us halfway to hell and back if we print."

I ask her to let Wheelie know. He has the misfortune to still be at his desk past eight thirty on a Friday night. Well, even if he were at home, we'd have to call him on this one.

The last thing Mal Wheelwright wants to do right now is deal with a story that is almost sure to earn us a lawsuit. Wheelie's had a rough day. When our new masters come in, they'll start lopping from the top. That's the way it always happens.

They'll want their own publisher, of course. And the publisher will want his own editor, who most likely won't be named Mal Wheelwright.

Whoever replaces Wheelie, of course, will probably take a look around the newsroom and decide who's too much of a drag on the company health insurance to merit keeping, but that could take awhile. Maybe, at thirty hours a week, I'll be seen as worth the trouble. With the new blood getting advice from our present publisher, though, I wouldn't buy stock in Willie Black right now.

I walk Wheelie through it. My proposed story would say that the man whose stolen plane destroyed two dozen of our residents at Dark Star appeared on the bay in 2000 from nobody-knows-where. It would further say that a man bearing a striking resemblance to Chopper Ware left Richmond at that time with no forwarding address and hasn't been heard from since. It would also note that the man who might be Chopper Ware had every reason in the world to despise the law firm of Bartley, Bowman and Bush, many of whose partners and staff were at Dark Star on that dark day.

"And he won't comment on whether it's him or not?"

I tell Wheelie again what Ware told me. I emphasize how angry he was, especially when I mentioned the photograph of Susanna.

"And you can't tell me for sure that this character is the same man that left here, that Patton guy?"

"Nothing's for sure, but this is about as sure as it gets."

I show Wheelie the newspaper article from the weekly paper, with Chopper Ware's picture. Then I show him the shots of James Patton, taken maybe a year earlier.

"Damn," Wheelie says. "Damn. It's got to be the same guy. But how can you prove it?"

I tell Wheelie there are ways, probably through tax records, but it will take awhile. I'm afraid somebody else will stumble on this.

"Maybe you should get the police involved with this."

It's about the last thing I want to do right now. If L.D. Jones gets a whiff of this, he'll either screw it up or leak it to the *Post* reporter who seems to now be his BFF.

I finally get Wheelie to agree to let me write it and see if we can get it past our soon-to-be-former publisher and our lawyers tomorrow.

In the meantime, I tell Wheelie I'll keep working the traps. I have a couple of ideas I'm not willing to share just yet.

Wheelie looks at the clock on the wall and curses. He's probably a couple of hours late getting home, and the news he's going to give his wife about his future employment will not be well-received.

I apologize for making a bad day a little worse.

"Don't sweat it," he says, patting me on the back. He lowers his voice.

"If you hear about any leads, you know, state jobs and such, I'd appreciate your letting me know. I figure you still have some contacts down there."

In a state capital, there are always jobs for people who can spell. Every state office seems to have its "media specialists," or whatever the hell they call them these days. Some of the jobs pay far better than what I'm making, probably better than what Wheelie's making even.

And some of the corporations really pay out the ass. The more reprehensible the product, the better "media specialist" pays. For the tobacco companies, the benefits can't be beat. Hell, maybe I should apply with one of those. I could give testimonials to their fine products, maybe even get free cigarettes.

There is a slight tradeoff though. You have to be willing to sing the company song, every single day. You have to be the one who stands up and lies through your teeth, if that's what it takes to protect your boss and "the brand." In short, you have to go from uncovering the news to covering it up.

Wheelie's got a wife and two kids.

I tell him I'll keep my ears open.

CHAPTER SIXTEEN

Saturday

"We need to talk" are the four words that most make me want to start running for the exit. I am not the world's biggest proponent of sharing feelings. Besides, all three of my divorces began with those four little words. "We need to talk," in my experience, means "I need to talk. You need to listen."

This time, though, when Cindy says the magic words, they're necessary.

With the sale of the paper finally a reality, and with the buyer being a chain that tends to care much more about its stockholders than its employees or its readers, and with my fifty-sixth birthday receding in the rearview mirror, Cindy can be excused for wondering what exactly the future holds for her, me, or us.

Everyone in the newsroom pretty much knows what they need to know about MediaWorld. We were all very busy last night, reading the tea leaves.

Several staffers had friends or acquaintances who work or did work for MediaWorld. Journalists tend to be a rather pessimistic group. That pessimism is hard-earned, gained from seeing on a daily basis just how mean, selfish, and dumb the world can be on the local, state, national, and international level. So you have to take the bitching with a grain of salt.

Still, what we heard did not make you comfortable with taking out a big mortgage.

No raises. Layoffs. A disregard for such trivialities as capital bureaus and copy desks. One former MediaWorld employee made us aware that five of the papers farther south now had one universal copy desk handling all the five papers' local copy. In other words, some worker bee two states away is supposed to know enough about your city to catch a reporter accidentally putting a house in the wrong part of town or getting the former mayor's name wrong, or forgetting to mention that he's a convicted felon.

Enos Jackson, who has been saving our butts for longer than I have been an adult, and has personally pulled mine from the fire on more than one occasion, looked a little green around the gills. The A personality types, the ones who go out and meet a million people while covering their beats, might have developed relationships that could lead to post-journalism PR jobs. Copy editors, who don't tend to know anybody much outside their neighborhoods or the newsroom and have a hard time looking you in the eye while they're lying to you, are what you might call screwed.

What the hell. From what I read on the blogs, where our readers weigh in on what they have allegedly read, most of our circulation has about a fifth-grade reading level anyhow. Maybe they won't notice when we go illiterate on them.

I told Enos to buck up, although I could think of no reason for him to do so. I did offer to buy him a drink or six after work. It was the best I could do.

So here Cindy and I sit, letting breakfast get cold and having the talk we apparently need.

"I'm going to have a job, come fall," she assures me. They do still need high school English teachers. Maybe now more than ever. The ones in the recent past apparently haven't done such a good job of imparting the intricacies of their native tongue to their students.

"We can get by," she says. "But we might have to think about moving somewhere else."

She has a point. It isn't like Kate is playing the wicked ex-wife. She's still making the mortgage payments on this place, in addition to paying the four-figure monthly condo fee that keeps the Prestwould, a grand dame with all the problems inherent in a 1929 building, up to twenty-first century standards. And I'm waiting to see if Kate is going to return to Green and Ellis. She's only fifteen days removed from her husband's death. Too soon to tell.

The problem is, I really have grown attached to this place. The neighbors, with very few exceptions (Feldman), are among the finest, kindest people I've ever lived around. We don't have a damn thing in common, for the most part. Many of them were born on third base, or at least second, while I was trying to just get out of the batter's box over on Oregon Hill. But they have taken me in as one of their own. This is the only place I've lived that I would truly hate to leave.

I tell Cindy we should wait a bit longer, to see which way the wind blows.

"Sounds like it's going to be blowing in your face, from what you say. Maybe we should start making other plans, just in case."

Since Cindy owns her now-unoccupied house, it's not like we don't have options. Still I like it here.

I take a bite of my lukewarm scrambled eggs and tell her that it's good to have a parachute, but that I'm still holding out hope.

"Well," she says, "just keep it in mind. You know, just in case."

OK, I hate change. Shoot me. You'd think a guy who burned through three marriages would be kind of flexible. Right now, though, I'm having trouble imagining a life that doesn't include a newsroom, or one in which I live somewhere other than where I am right now. Cindy is a bit lighter on her feet. She's probably a lot more sensible. Sensible people don't invest their lives in print journalism.

We haven't used the m-word. We're happy as clams living in sin, so why rock the boat? However, I sometimes wonder if Cindy's reluctance is because she's satisfied with the status quo, or because her first marriage ended so badly that she never wants to walk down the aisle again, or because she's afraid the mere mention of it would send me running for the front door.

We need to talk.

Before I went home last night, and before having too many beers with Enos Jackson and other uneasy coworkers, I wrote the first draft of what I hope will be an A1 story in Sunday's paper.

I've portrayed Chopper Ware as a man of mystery. God knows, the up-to-date photo of him that Sarah took when we were down there last week does nothing to undercut that image. In the small space between his hat and his white beard, his eyes have that 500-yard stare you see sometimes in Civil War photographs or shots of soldiers just back from hell.

I've included the censored version of his rather loud and violent reaction to my questions about James Patton, since nothing he said was off the record. I have put the pieces out there, leaving it to our readers to connect the dots. There's nothing in the story about Ware's fishing trip the afternoon of April 8.

Today I have a couple of goals, other than chronicling whatever carnage develops in Richmond on this fine spring day.

First, I want to do all I can to make sure that the story gets into tomorrow's paper. Maybe the fact that our publisher is a short-timer will make her more amenable to running with a story that screams "sue us." I can only hope.

Second, I need to make a run by the 7-Eleven. I'm almost out of Camels, and I'm thinking the store across from the Devil's Triangle might be just the place to go shopping.

Second things first. I make my way through the Fan, dodging the joggers who choose to spurn perfectly good sidewalks and the bicyclists who think they own the goddamn street. The latter keep me going a stately fifteen miles an hour. Then, when they get to a stoplight, they glance both ways and then run it, leaving me behind to think dark thoughts.

I park across from the crash site. The 7-Eleven has a new sign, again thanking heaven for itself.

Inside the place is quiet, as I would expect at ten on a Saturday morning. I buy my cigarettes and strike up a conversation with the clerk. She's a VCU student who, like most of her classmates, has to work her buns off just to pay her tuition. She indicates that she is not planning on making a career in the convenience-store field.

A quick look around tells me what I need to know. The surveillance camera is situated so that anyone robbing this pretty clerk would get his picture in the paper pretty soon. But what I was looking for and found was the one pointed across the parking lot, presumably to videotape thieves as they made their short-lived getaway.

I ask her if the cops have shown any interest in the surveillance cameras.

"Oh, yeah," she says, probably happy to have something else to do besides sell single beers and hand out lottery tickets to people who get by on booze and hope. "They took them I think the day after the crash. I wasn't here, thank God, when it happened. I was gone, like all that weekend. But Amir told me about it."

"And they didn't return them?"

She shrugs her shoulders. I back away and let a man in thrift-shop casual put his last twenty dollars on MegaMillions.

The clerk says Amir, the manager, won't be back until Monday. I have what might be a better idea though. I thank her for her time and, what the hell, buy a two-dollar lottery ticket.

On the way out, I see my old friend Cottonmouth. His eyes light up when he spots a familiar wallet. I give him the lottery ticket and wish him luck. I think he'd rather have had the two bucks.

PEACHY LOVE's car is parked outside her house, and I don't see a vehicle with Maryland plates in the vicinity, so I assume Wendell is elsewhere.

It would not go well if Cindy saw me going into or coming out of Peachy Love's abode. She might suspect that we've "seen" each other in the not-so-distant past. I've tried to dispel any thoughts that the past is not past.

Peachy looks both ways and then quickly ushers me in the front door. As much shit as I'd be in if I was seen slipping unescorted into Peachy's place, she'd be in more. L.D. Jones would give up his year-end bonus to find who keeps slipping information to the "nosy-ass press."

She asks me what I want.

"A little sugar, maybe?"

Peachy isn't really trying to get me in the sack. She's just having fun with an old friend, I'm sure.

I tell her I'm afraid I might get diabetes if I stayed around her too long.

"Well," she says, "something's gonna get you. Might as well be something sweet."

We eventually dispense with the bullshit. I tell her why I'm here.

"Oh, yeah," she says. "They gave that tape a thorough look-see, I'm pretty sure. I heard they went back a couple of hours."

"On the one in the store and the one in the parking lot?"

"Yeah. Both, I think."

"And they didn't find anything worth following up on?"

"If they had," Peachy says, "I'm sure we'd all have heard about it by now. I don't know if they really were that into checking the tapes anyhow. Seems like it's pretty cut-and-dried. Nut crashes plane."

I ask her if the police still have the tapes.

"They probably do. Probably still in the evidence room."

"And how does one get into the evidence room?"

"One doesn't," she says, "unless one is a cop."

"Or a media relations person employed by the cops."

"Oh, no. You're not getting me involved in this."

I explain what I'm looking for.

She whistles and shakes her head.

"Damn, that's a hell of a yarn. Why don't you just go in and tell the chief what you told me?"

I tell her that, first, I don't think L.D. Jones is speaking to me these days. Second, I doubt they'd take it very seriously, considering that I'm basically working on hunches at this point.

"They won't think anything about you going back there, and all you have to do is put those tapes in your pocket and walk out," I tell her.

"And walk them back in later too."

What turns the tide in my favor, I think, is that Peachy is still a journalist at heart. She's making good, safe money working for the police, but part of her wants to be back at the paper, chasing the biggest story in town.

Either that, or the chief has managed to piss her off as badly as he has me.

She says she'll see what she can do.

"Today?" I ask her, really pushing it now.

She sighs and says now is as good a time as any. It's no more than ten minutes from Peachy's to the precinct. I tell her I can wait. She says that'll be OK, as long as I don't go outside. She says the less anybody sees my ass around here, the better.

So I wait. I can't smoke, but I do borrow one of Peachy's Miller High Lifes.

She's back within forty-five minutes.

"The little shithead who's minding property today didn't even ask for ID when I walked in," she says. "I was ready to give him some cock-and-bull story about research, but he just waved me through. Didn't even look up from the porn he was looking at on his computer."

She reaches in her coat pocket and pulls out two tapes.

I thank her profusely. She reminds me that if I don't have the tapes back to her by noon tomorrow, so she can return them to their rightful place, I will wish I had.

"This is really a shot in the dark," she tells me.

"I know. I've been wrong before. But if you don't shoot, you don't hit anything."

She reminds me that I have been right on occasion too. I thank her for the confidence boost.

On the way out, I promise to be on her doorstep at noon tomorrow.

She says she's starting to get a little paranoid. She suggests that I go out the back door and down the alley, then return to my car via the side street.

"And tomorrow, just meet me somewhere."

I suggest eleven forty-five at the 7-Eleven parking lot.

"Scene of the crime," she says.

But what crime exactly is what I'm wondering.

After lunch I clock in and start my campaign to get what I know so far, or think I know, in the paper.

At some point, I must have turned off my cell phone. When I check it, there's a message from Chopper Ware.

"I've contacted my lawyer down here," he says. "We're all ready to sue your ass just as soon as I see one damn word about what you talked about yesterday. As a matter of fact, he's probably already been in touch with your publisher. You think you can just run over me, but you're about to find out you can't."

The second message is from my publisher. Her version of "we need to talk" is "see me."

Wheelie is in, looking a little haggard, like he didn't sleep so well last night.

I ask him if the publisher is in. He says she is, and the way he says it, grabbing his coat at the same time, I'm sure he knows what this is all about.

Ms. Dominick is indeed in on a Saturday. When we climb the stairs, her office is the only one on the suit floor that is occupied. To find her compatriots, try the Country Club of Virginia's James River course.

There is a box beside Dominick's desk, and she's putting some mementoes into it, mostly awards and other stuff from her earlier vocation and true love, advertising.

"You're not going to let me get out of here easy, are you, Willie?" she says.

"I thought you were going to be here to give the new broom some guidance."

She laughs.

"That was all bullshit. If the geniuses at MediaWorld want guidance, they know where they can find me. I'm just waiting to see what the big boys want me to do next. You're not going to miss me, are you, Willie?"

That one doesn't rate a comment.

She sighs.

"OK. Make your pitch. Why should we run whatever the hell you've written and get our butts sued?"

I hand her the printout. She tells Wheelie and me to get a cup of coffee or something and come back in ten minutes.

"What do you think our chances are?" I ask Wheelie.

He shrugs.

"She's in kind of a weird mood, like maybe she's slipping out of boss mode and becoming human again."

"Again?"

This is about as close as my editor will come to ragging on Dominick. You've got to respect him for that. If I've caught a peck of crap from here, Wheelie's been on the receiving end of a couple of bushels.

We give her ten minutes and a couple more for good measure, then go back in.

We sit. She doesn't say anything at first. Then she picks up what I've written so far and more or less waves it at me.

"This guy," she says, "this Chopper Ware, he says he'll sue us to hell and back if we run this."

She pauses, I think for dramatic effect.

"What I want to know is, are you sure about this? I mean, about him and this Patton character being the same man?"

I tell her that I am 99 percent sure. When some people say they're 99 percent sure, it just means they're mostly sure. When I say it, it means that there is only one chance in a hundred that I'm wrong. I stress this to the publisher.

"So the guy gets worked over by BB&B after his daughter's death, and then he wins a lawsuit and disappears, and now two people say he and this Chopper Ware, whose plane was stolen, are one and the same. Amazing if true."

I tell her that I am pursuing other leads. Sarah's trying to find something that will make it a lead-pipe cinch that Ware is Patton. I don't mention the 7-Eleven tapes, not until I've seen them and know if I'm barking up the wrong tree.

"If you're wrong," she says, "or even if you can't prove you're right, this paper, or rather MediaWorld, is going to be writing a hell of a check. They might even take a little out of our personal hides."

She puts the printout down. She looks at me.

"Are you absolutely sure that you're 99 percent sure?"

I tell her that, yes, I am that sure.

"Aw, fuck it," she says finally. "Let me run it past the lawyer, if he's sober enough to read. When the shit hits the fan, MediaWorld can deal with it."

She gets up to take another plastic press association plaque off the wall, which is our cue to get the hell out of there before she changes her mind.

"Man," Wheelie says as soon as we're out of earshot, "I can't believe she did that."

I'm a little stunned myself, but maybe he's right. Maybe the dragon lady is ready to shed her skin and go onto her next assignment. Maybe, like they teach you in MBA school, it was all just business.

I POLISH my story and hand it over to Wheelie, who sends it along to the publisher, who forwards it to the mouthpiece whose job it is to keep us from losing lawsuits.

He has a lot of questions, but he, too, eventually signs off on it. Maybe he figures the new boys will bring in their own lawyer, and so he's not quite as motivated to do due diligence as he was before yesterday's announcement. Maybe it's just Saturday afternoon and he has better things to do.

I need some time to be alone with the tapes Peachy borrowed for me. I tell Sally as much as I feel comfortable telling her about what I suspect, and she says she'll have somebody cover for me for the next four or five hours. She's as surprised as Wheelie and I were to discover that we're going to actually run what I've written about James Patton and Chopper Ware.

"If we're going to run it," she says, "we need to run it big."

Wheelie agrees, and a blockbuster profile of the new city manager that was going to be atop A1 gets pushed back to Monday.

It seems only fair that I call Chopper Ware, just so he'll know to buy a Sunday paper. However, I have some binge-watching to do first.

Ed Chenowith helps me set up the VCR player. I insert the tape that focuses on the front counter. The tape is good for a day, midnight to midnight. Peachy thinks the cops only looked at the hour or two leading up to the crash, which makes sense, I guess. That would take them back to about three thirty. Apparently they didn't find anything noteworthy.

I go back a bit farther, to noon, and start fast-forwarding. Nothing much catches my eye for what seems like an eternity. I have to stop the damn thing twice so I can blink.

Then something catches my eye. I go back and play it at normal speed. I play it again.

"Son of a bitch."

It's eight o'clock by the time I resurface in the newsroom. The night is quiet so far, crime-wise, but the heavy hitters won't come out until a few hours from now.

I call Chopper Ware on his cell phone. To my surprise, he answers. It sounds like he's in a bar. I wish I was.

I don't see any sense in pulling punches at this point. I tell him about the tapes I've just watched.

"Chopper," I tell him, "we need to talk."

CHAPTER SEVENTEEN

Sunday

Last night, before I gave Chopper Ware the lowdown on the tape I saw, I informed him, as a matter of courtesy, that we would be running my story about James Patton, and that he could sue if he wanted to. Chopper didn't seem to appreciate my courtesy, and when I explained why we needed to have a serious conversation ASAP, he did not take it well.

The whiskey or whatever was doing the talking for the first couple of minutes, but then Chopper got past the booze and realized what I was telling him and why he needed to listen.

"That don't prove a damn thing," he said after his spleen had been properly vented. "I've seen them cameras. We've got one in my store. The pictures are fuzzy as hell."

I assure him that I have seen enough to be sure, especially on top of what I know already.

"I already told you I was out fishing that day."

"By yourself."

"What if I wasn't fishing?" he said after a pause. "I sure as hell wasn't anywhere near Richmond."

That, I told him, is a matter that is up for debate.

"If you're so damn sure, why don't you call the police?"

I said I'd rather hear it from him, but that I could call the cops, if that's what he wanted. I was bluffing. I had no intention of telling L.D. Jones anything for the time being.

Ware didn't say anything for so long I thought he had hung up.

Then: "OK. So you want to talk. When?"

I told him tomorrow. He said tomorrow would be fine. We set it up for one thirty. Against all odds, Chopper Ware claims to be a churchgoer.

SATURDAY NIGHT was going so well. Then, as is so often the case, a couple of knuckleheads ruined it for me. I was almost out the door when we got word of a possible homicide on the North Side, on Brook Road.

A bicyclist tooling along that somewhat busy thoroughfare apparently thought a passing car came a little too close for comfort. He yelled something at the guy. Usually that's the end of it. But the driver, who not surprisingly had just come from a bar, had his windows down, enjoying the warm spring night. He heard what the cyclist called him. He took umbrage.

According to the cyclist, the only one around to tell the story, the driver pulled his car slowly into the bike lane and got out of his car. The cyclist said he could have gone around the car, taken off, and avoided confrontation, but he figured the guy would just get back behind the wheel and run him down.

And that's where it got a little weird. Normally you'd think the drunk guy in the car would be the one who was packing. He did have a gun in the car, like apparently everybody else in this ammo-addicted town, but he neglected to take it with him when he got out to teach the cyclist some manners.

No, it was the cyclist who came to a fistfight with a gun. He apparently had one in his backpack, and it was loaded. So when the would-be badass in the car stepped out and started walking toward him, promising great violence (again, according to the cyclist), he whipped it out and plugged him.

He only shot him once, but he was either lucky or unlucky, according to your viewpoint. Bulls-eye. Right in the heart.

By the time I got there, the cyclist, who looked the way most of them do—about 140 vegan pounds soaking wet—was leaning against the car of the guy he'd just shot and killed. He was handcuffed, headed for the bowels of our legal system. He appeared to be a little stunned.

I am sure that one of our idiot legislators will hop on this and present a bill defending the right of all bicyclists to conceal-carry.

And so I got to write the city's first cycling road-rage homicide story. Certainly one for the scrapbook. It makes me think I should resist the urge I sometimes have to give the slow-ass cyclist in front of me a little love tap with my Honda. Who knew vegans could be so violent? I guess kale will do that to you.

Most of the details were for our online edition since I had about twenty minutes from the time I got to the scene until final lockup. By the time I came home, it was almost two, and I hadn't even had time to pay my respects at Penny Lane.

I had planned to make a quick appearance at the Oregon Hill gang's breakfast at Joe's, since I was supposed to be down at Topping by one thirty, and I have to return the tapes to Peachy at eleven forty-five. There was no need to tell Cindy about what I saw on the tape yesterday. She might worry.

Then I got a call about nine thirty from Chopper Ware. He was almost civil, asking if we could please put off our little meeting until tomorrow morning. He said he could prove to me then that he was nowhere near Richmond on the afternoon of April 8.

"You know all hell has broke loose down here," he said. "I've gotten I bet ten phone calls already. You've stirred up a shit storm for me."

There was something in his tone, almost like a whine, and I was pretty sure Chopper wasn't going to be siccing his lawyer on us.

So we set up a meeting for nine tomorrow. I wisely requested that we meet at a public place. I suggested the diner in Kilmarnock where I've been a couple of times already, and he seemed good with that.

WHEN CINDY, Abe, and I get to Joe's, R.P. and Andy are already there. It is heartening, as I walk toward the back booth, to see a handful of people actually reading the paper. Of course, they all appear to be AARP-eligible. "Where is James Patton?/ (and who is James Ware?)" screams the two-deck headline at the top of A1. "Cyclist shoots, kills motorist" whispers the one in the box at the bottom.

"You've been a busy boy," R.P. says. "They aren't paying you enough."

When I tell my old Hill buddies that I'm doing this for thirty hours pay instead of forty these days, they are somewhat mystified. Most people, it seems, work to make money. Giving 110 percent for 25 percent less pay doesn't make much sense to them. Hell, it doesn't make much sense to me either, when I think about it. But what else is a nicotine addict in his mid-fifties with authority issues going to do?

We've hogged the table through about three cups of coffee each, a dozen or so three-dollar Bloody Marys, and enough unhealthy food to last us until supper when I feel my cell phone vibrating in my pocket.

L.D. Jones is gracing me with a call.

I'm kind of surprised that he waited this long. I went to sleep last night half expecting the chief to give me a wake-up call as soon as he had a chance to read my story.

Maybe the chief is slowing down.

"What the hell is this?" he inquires. I hold the phone away from my ear and then excuse myself so I can talk to L.D. in a more private setting, where perhaps I can yell back at him. Also, if I go outside, maybe I can sneak in a Camel.

"Why didn't you tell me something about all this?" he says, after I make him wait while I light up. "If you've got some half-assed theory, why do you have to spread it all over the front page? Why didn't you come to me?"

I remind L.D. that I don't decide story placement and that he hasn't been so good about sharing in the recent or even distant past. I further remind him that I've come to him with alternative theories related to police business before and been cruelly rebuffed.

"You can't just throw shit like that out there without any proof," he says. "It's reckless. And you're interfering with my investigation."

"What investigation? You guys have this one already figured out, right? Crazy man crashes plane, kills two dozen. End of story."

"We're still looking into it," he says.

"Ongoing investigation."

"Damn straight. And you're interfering with it."

I know the chief. He doesn't care that I'm butting in, but he'd like to be informed so he can claim credit for himself and his people in case something as yet unearthed comes to light. I understand that. It always looks bad when somebody other than the police gets to the bottom first.

He asks me what exactly I think "this Ware guy" has to do with what happened at Dark Star.

"I mean, it was his plane, but he wasn't flying the damn thing."

I tell L.D. that I don't know if he had anything to do with anything. I was just pointing out that the guy whose plane made a parking lot out of one of our local eateries looked a lot like a guy who had a longstanding grudge against some of the people who got incinerated when that plane made an untimely landing.

I don't tell L.D. about the tapes, the ones that were "borrowed" from his office and are in my pocket at present. That could prove a bit sticky. I still don't know how I'm going to explain how I saw those tapes when and if that bit of information sees daylight. I'll cross that rickety bridge later.

The chief says he wants to talk to Chopper Ware, and I'm hoping he doesn't get around to that until sometime after tomorrow.

I ask him if the police have been able to figure out anything about David Biggio's last phone call, the one to or from the plane.

He says there was nothing to find out, no way of tracing it. The chief figures it was a wrong number.

"From a throwaway phone?"

"Everything that happens isn't some kind of goddamn clue. You think real life is like *Law and Order* or one of those damn murder mysteries my wife likes to read."

No, I tell him, I don't think everything is a clue, but sometimes something is.

L.D. doesn't say anything.

I make him an offer.

"Can you do something for me tomorrow?"

He is literally sputtering.

"Why the fuck would I do something for you, other than throw your ass in jail for obstruction of justice?"

I explain that I have other information, information that could reopen the Dark Star case with a vengeance, but that I have to do it my way. However, I tell him, if you do something for me, I promise to let you know what I've found out, even before I put it in print. I can tell our readers that their faithful reporter was acting on an anonymous tip from someone high in the police hierarchy when he stumbled on the truth about what happened April 8.

"That sounds like a lot of hoodoo bullshit to me," he says. L.D. knows, though, that I've always played straight with him, either giving him the truth or nothing. No lies. I wish the same were true about his end of the relationship, but a chief's got to do what a chief's got to do.

I tell him what I want. He says he'll see what he can do. Hell, it can't hurt to ask.

I finish my smoke and go back inside, where my friends are settling up.

Cindy isn't too happy when I drop her off at the Prestwould and tell her I have a couple of stops to make before we commence with the rest of the day she has planned for us, which I fear involves seeing a movie in which there is a lot of conversation and nothing gets blown up.

"Maybe I should just get one of the girls to go with me," she says. I sense that agreeing with her would not be in my best long-term interests. I promise to be back as quickly as I can. I do not mention either Peachy Love or my other destination.

I MAKE it to the 7-Eleven parking lot at eleven forty-five on the nose. Peachy is already there, sitting in her car, kind of slumped down in the seat so nobody will see her.

I park next to her and slip into the passenger seat, handing her the tapes.

"This place wasn't the best idea in the world," she says. "Scrunch down a little in the seat there."

A least two cop cars have driven by, she tells me.

"I thought one of them was going to pull in, and then where would I be?"

"You'd just tell the guy you came here to buy a 40 to drink on the way home."

"You're just full of good ideas, aren't you?"

She's also been panhandled twice, by guys walking right up to her window. Looking around, I don't think either of them was Cottonmouth.

"When I showed them my police ID, they kinda backed away."

She looks around again to make sure none of her compatriots are in the vicinity.

"So did you find what you were looking for?"

I swear her to secrecy and tell her what I found.

"You really, really ought to be giving this to the police," Peachy says, frowning at me. "I mean, this is some serious shit."

One more day, I promise her, and all will be revealed.

I thank her again and promise to express my appreciation in a more substantive way sometime soon. I'm thinking about something along the lines of dinner at Lemaire for her and Wendell.

When Peachy smirks and says she's sure I'll think of something, she could be imputing me with baser thoughts.

As I slip out of her car, she puts her right hand on my left one.

"Be careful," she advises me. "We don't need some amateur detective getting his ass killed."

My next stop on this lovely Sunday is another clandestine location.

On a hunch, I gave Louisa Klassen my e-mail address the last time I saw her and told her to call me if she remembered anything.

The message she left me sometime last night, the one I saw after I got up this morning, only said "need to talk tomorrow. can do 12 or 1 pm. Don't call."

So I e-mailed her back: "Chiocca's. 12:30." She sent back "OK," so here I am, walking into what used to be one of my favorite hangouts. I don't know why it still isn't, to tell you the truth. Cold beer, great sandwiches, lots of your basic local color. It's the kind of dark, low-ceilinged place down a flight of stone steps where I can lose an afternoon or an evening and then ruin my buzz by busting my ass on those steps on the way out.

Louisa is sitting in one of the cramped booths, drinking a cup of coffee. Hell, I didn't know they served anything nonalcoholic in here. I order a beer, just to be sociable.

I slip in opposite her. She looks nervous, but then she pretty much always looks nervous, the times I've seen her.

It turns out that Bobby's gone on a camping trip with his buddies and won't likely be back until sometime midafternoon or later.

"There's something I need to tell you," she says. "I didn't mention it before, but it's bothering me."

I do what I do best. I shut up.

"I talked to him."

"Him?"

"David."

I am, as they say, all ears.

On Wednesday, two days before the Dark Star crash, David Biggio called his ex-wife.

"I hadn't talked to him in I don't know how long," she says. "Maybe five years. At first I figured it was because of the injunction. But then I wondered if he hadn't gone off somewhere and, you know, died. And then Arthur Heutz ran into him."

She says she thought about hanging up on her ex, but she didn't.

"He told me about the insurance policy."

She says she didn't mention it before, mainly because her ex-husband told her not to.

"He said it was something he wanted to leave Brandy, all he could leave her. But he said it shouldn't look like it was something I knew about beforehand, that it'd be better if I acted like I was surprised."

"He didn't say anything about crashing a plane, did he?"

She puts her hands on the coffee cup, like she's trying to warm them up.

"No. He never said anything like that. If he had, I'd have told him not to do it, I swear. He just said Brandy might be able to cash in on it sometime soon."

She looks like she's about to cry.

"I should've asked him more questions. I knew something was wrong. But, to tell you the truth, I just wanted to get him off the phone. I really, really didn't want to have anything more to do with David. That part of my life is something I'd like to leave behind."

I ask her if he said anything about how much the policy was for.

"He told me it was half a million dollars. I didn't believe him, but he wasn't lying. Of course, we're never going to see any of that now."

I want to tell her "we," meaning her and Bobby, shouldn't be seeing any of it anyhow. David Biggio meant it to be for the daughter who was taken away from him.

"Did he say how he paid for that policy? Seems like it'd be a little expensive."

"Oh, he said not to worry about that, that a rich friend was taking care of all that for him. I said something like 'that must be some kind of friend,' and he kind of laughed and said 'yeah, he's a good one, all right.' "

I ask Louisa if he mentioned the friend's name.

She pauses and says that he did.

"It was Jimmy something. I can't remember the last name."

I thank her for sharing.

"This isn't going to get me in any trouble, is it?" she asks me. Her hand brushes her coffee, almost knocking it over. She's had two cups since I've been here, and they haven't made her any less jittery.

I tell her that it's unlikely. After all, she had no way to know David Biggio was going to do what he did. She might have been a little suspicious, I think but don't say, but they can't put you in jail for what you don't know.

She might have to answer a few questions for the police, I suggest, when everything comes out, but it might not even come to that. It all depends on what happens tomorrow.

She says that I might want to leave first. I put down a five for the beer and start to slide out of the booth.

She puts her hand out to stop me.

"Do you really think he did it?" she says. "On purpose, I mean. I can't wrap my head around why he'd do such a thing. Those people never did anything to him, that anybody knows about."

"Well, you hadn't seen him in a long time. Maybe he got worse."

There's no sense in telling Louisa anything else right now. She's probably got her hands full dealing with an asshole husband who will be coming back home too soon hung over and pissed off about the fortune he lost, the one that he never was entitled to in the first place.

WE MAKE it to the three o'clock showing of a movie about the terrible twists and turns a couple must endure between "meeting cute" and accepting the inevitability of true and everlasting love.

The popcorn was good.

CHAPTER EIGHTEEN

Monday

We talked a bit about "sharing" when we got home from the movie yesterday. Cindy has learned enough about my past to know that I suck at this particular concept.

I'll share my money, my time, my house, the shirt off my back if that's what it takes to make a friend's life a little easier. Sharing what's inside, though, is another matter.

What, Cindy asked, are you thinking? That's what she wants to know. What do you know that you're keeping locked up?

I nodded and made appropriate noises. She's probably right. Maybe I ought to let her know what I have planned for today on my little jaunt down to Topping. She's plugged in enough, since she's been down there with me already, to know that something is looming offshore like those Nor'easters that catch us unaware once or twice a year.

But I didn't tell her everything. The excuse I give myself is that I don't want her to worry. There is a certain amount of risk involved here, although I am trying to keep it to a minimum.

Maybe no man is an island, but I have a lifetime habit of keeping a tiny little atoll inside my fevered brain as my own private sanctuary. I know it's a piece of land I must cede if I'm going to finally have a relationship with a woman that lasts longer than a new pair of Docksiders, but old habits die hard.

I called Sarah Goodnight about eight last night, to see if she had found out anything else concerning the good Mr. Ware. She said she hadn't, and she asked me whether I had any new information.

I told her that I did and that I would tell her all about it as soon as I made one more trip down to Topping. She asked me if she could come with me. Well, she didn't ask. She demanded.

"Dammit, Willie, I've been working this story too. You're keeping me in the dark."

Like Cindy, she'd like to see me share a little. I tell her that the only way Chopper Ware agreed to have this very serious and potentially life-altering conversation with me was if I came alone. That's a lie, but there isn't any sense in putting a perfectly good reporter, one whose future I care about, in harm's way.

I told her that I'll be safe, that we're having our little tête-à-tête over breakfast at the diner in Kilmarnock, out in the open with plenty of witnesses.

She wasn't very happy when she hung up. I hope she will see the method in my madness when it all shakes out.

I LEAVE the Prestwould at seven fifteen. Cindy wakes up long enough to kiss me good-bye and tell me to be careful. The look she gives me when she says it lets me know that she's aware I'm still not sharing.

I bolt before we can talk some more.

I'm not even out to I-95 when the cell phone rings. I see who it is and pull off Belvidere onto a side street in Jackson Ward.

"I've got something on that Patton guy," L.D. Jones says when I answer.

It turns out that the chief is not much on sharing either. Prior to our chat yesterday, the police got a call from a guy about the story on James Patton and Chopper Ware in yesterday's editions.

"He said he tried to get in touch with you all at the paper, but nobody answered the phone," L.D. says. I think I hear him chuckle. Once again, our penny-wise, otherwise-foolish austerity has cost us a valuable tip.

The call was from a guy out in Chesterfield County. When he told the poor sap handling the phones at police headquarters that he was James Patton's first cousin, the call eventually got patched through to a detective.

What he told the detective was that he had been in touch with James Patton, or at least got a Christmas card from him, only four years ago.

"The guy said he had given Patton up for dead. They used to be close, almost like brothers, he said, when they were kids. But after Patton got the settlement from that boy's family, he just disappeared."

And then, four years ago, the cousin got a card. He said his wife keeps old Christmas cards, or at least ones from people they don't see that often. He had rummaged through the attic and found the one she'd saved from James Patton.

He gave it to the detective, and L.D. says he's looking at it right now.

"It says, 'Long time, no see. You might not hear from me again. Just wanted you to know I'm well.' "

"That's it?"

"Nah. He sent a two-page newsletter about his year too, along with pictures and a link to his website."

The chief is capable of humor, it seems.

"No return address?"

"Right."

"How about a postmark?"

He tells me what I need to know.

"Now," he says, "it's time for you to cough up a little information for me, a little of the old quid pro quo."

"I wasn't aware you knew Latin."

"What the fuck are you talking about?"

I give him the particulars of the favor I asked of him yesterday. I give him the address for the diner in Kilmarnock.

"Have somebody there at ten thirty. Not after, and not before."

"You're supposed to tell me what the hell you're doing," he says. "That was the promise."

I will, I say, in about three hours.

The chief isn't happy with that arrangement. He would be even less happy if he found out that I "borrowed" tapes from the police evidence room.

It has occurred to me that if everything works out the way I want it to, it might be necessary for L.D. to know what's on those tapes, farther back than his minions bothered to look. Since the guy on Saturday duty and the one Sunday might remember that Peachy made visits those two days, I have to find a way to protect her—and to save an invaluable source, I might add.

There is a solution. Gillespie to the rescue.

GILLESPIE'S NO detective. He probably couldn't solve the Kidspot puzzle on the comics page. I'm about to give him his big chance.

Before I left the parking lot this morning, I called him on his cell. He wasn't that happy to hear from me, but at least his ass was awake.

I told him that I had a conversation with a clerk at the 7-Eleven, and I suggested that our chat indicated that a really squared-away cop could do himself a lot of good by taking a better look at the tapes the police seized from the store the day of the crash.

"Go back maybe four hours," I told him. "See what you find."

Gillespie is not quick on the uptake. When I told him that there might be a promotion for someone wise enough to heed my advice, he grunted and said he'd see what he could do.

"Gillespie," I told him, "you need to get on this right now, because it might be old news in four or five hours. And when they want to know where you got the tip from prior to giving you a medal, it better not be me."

In order to put the strongest possible emphasis on it, I told him the tip I had just given him was worth more than all the donuts at the Sugar Shack.

WHEN I pull into the parking lot at the diner, I don't see Chopper Ware's big-ass truck. There is a van, though, with the name of his hardware store on the side of it.

Inside the diner I don't see Ware at first, but then I spy a Panama hat perched atop a nest of white hair in the rear booth, facing the back of the place.

When I sit down facing him, he's reading the local weekly. He doesn't look up or otherwise acknowledge my existence. The same woman who waited on me before comes to take my order.

"Hey," she says. "You again. You planning on moving down here, or what?"

I tell her that I'm just passing through. I order coffee and scrambled eggs.

Finally Chopper carefully folds the paper and looks up.

"So," he says, "what do you think you've got?"

I tell him that all I have at present are a lot of seemingly unrelated facts that might or might not turn out to be relevant.

"Cut the bullshit. Just spit it out."

His voice is a low rumble, like distant thunder. There's nobody within two booths of us, but Chopper's being cautious.

So I start small.

"Those photos, for openers. If you're not James Patton, you've got a lot of folks fooled."

He laughs.

"A lot of people look alike. That doesn't prove anything."

"Well, we're working on some other stuff, trying to pin it down."

The waitress brings my coffee. He waits until she's left.

"Just as a for-instance," he says, "why would it matter even if you did find out that I was this James Patton? I mean, was he wanted for murder or something? I read your story, and I don't see that it's any of your goddamn business who I am or am not."

I note that if he is James Patton, he certainly had all the reason in the world to have a very large beef with the law firm of Bartley, Bowman and Bush, the same firm that his plane decimated.

"My plane, flown by a nut who stole it from me."

A woman in a floppy hat and sunglasses comes into the diner, looks around, and then leaves. Otherwise I count five people in the place.

"And that photo of Susanna Patton. I'd be willing to bet that the girl in the picture I saw in your office is her identical twin."

His right hand clenches into a fist. Then he relaxes and forces a laugh.

I press on.

"Then there was the Christmas card."

He's not ready for this one.

"The what?"

"The Christmas card. The one James Patton sent his cousin four years ago. Said something about how he was safe but that the cousin wouldn't be hearing from him again."

"What the hell's that got to do with anything?"

"Well, it didn't have a return address, but it did have a postmark."

He sighs. He doesn't have to ask what the postmark was.

"Then there's the life-insurance policy."

"Shit. We've been over that already. So he put me down as a contact when he bought the policy. So what?"

"Well, it's a little more complicated than that."

My scrambled eggs come. I take a couple of bites and wipe my mouth. I'm in no hurry. I'm kind of enjoying this, in a perverse kind of way. Chopper Ware is not.

"Tell me about 'complicated,'" he says. He seems like he's trying to control his temper.

So I tell him about Louisa Klassen, David Biggio's ex-wife, who remembers that her ex-husband said the premium on that half-million-dollar insurance policy was bought for him by a good friend, a rich guy named Jimmy.

"I remember you saying that Biggio was the only one down here who called you Jimmy instead of Chopper."

"So what? There are a lot of Jimmys down here, and I bet one or two of 'em are a hell of a lot better off than me. Hell, calling me 'rich' is a stretch, don't you think?"

I keep eating. He waits until I finish my eggs before he asks the question I know he's dying to ask.

"So what's in it for you? Is this a damn shakedown or something? You want me to pay you to go away?"

I doubt if Chopper Ware would understand if I told him that I only wanted to break the story of the year in our circulation area, that I was doing this on one of my three days off, for a paper that had just cut my hours by one-fourth.

I just tell him that money is not involved.

"Good," he says, "because you ain't going to get any. You listen to me: You can try to prove that I'm this Patton fella, which I doubt you will, and I'll just say I wanted to start over, that I had suffered terrible losses and just wanted to have a fresh start as somebody new. Hell, folks will feel sorry for me. They might make me the marshal in the Christmas parade."

The waitress refills our coffee.

"If that's all there was," I tell Chopper, "I wouldn't have wasted time and gas coming down here."

And so I explain about the tapes.

"You really should have worn some kind of disguise," I tell him. "Those photos might not be conclusive, but the man who bought that throwaway cell phone from the 7-Eleven a little over three hours before your plane went boom? I'd swear that guy is James 'Chopper' Ware."

The cherry on top, I tell him, is the tape of the parking lot. There can't be a lot of monster trucks like his rolling around Richmond, and I'm sure the cops, once they get around to looking all the way back on those tapes, will be able to zoom in and read the license plate.

"You told me you were out fishing. I think you were in Richmond all afternoon."

Chopper's face is almost as pale as his hair by now. He waits for me to continue.

"Somebody made a phone call to Biggio, in your plane, not five minutes before it crashed. They used a throwaway phone.

The closest place to Dark Star that sells those phones is that 7-Eleven across the street.

"You see where it looks kind of suspicious."

"So what? You think I was flying that plane by remote control, or maybe I hypnotized Biggio and made him kill all those people?"

"Not exactly."

It's time to lay out my theory, one I haven't even shared with L.D. Jones. It would have sounded too wacky to me if somebody had pitched it to me a week ago.

"Let's talk about David Biggio's favorite lawyer, one that wasn't in Dark Star that afternoon because he was dead at the time."

I ask Chopper if he can prove where he was the evening of the fifth, the night Thomas Jackson Bonesteel was murdered.

"Why should I?"

"We already know that Biggio wasn't there, at least according to his friend with benefits. The man most likely to have dispatched Bonesteel was all tucked in here in Kilmarnock.

"But where were you?"

Chopper's eyes are big as saucers behind his glasses.

"What the hell would I want to kill some lawyer I didn't even know? I never met him."

"No. That's probably right. And I'd bet that David Biggio never met any of those lawyers who died in Dark Star that Friday."

He says he doesn't know what I'm getting at, but I'm pretty damn sure he does.

"You know what really tipped me off?" I ask him.

Chopper says he's dying to hear.

"It was the initials. It finally hit me, after I heard about how your daughter died. Somebody took the trouble to carve SAP on Bonesteel's chest, before or after he died. The cops wondered if it was some statement about the deceased, like he was a sap. But it just came to me: Susanna Alford Patton."

"You can't prove shit," Chopper says, with very little conviction.

I bluff a little, telling him that the cops were able to get some prints of tire tracks in the mud outside Bonesteel's house. They haven't been able to match them so far, but I'm betting that with a little help they will.

I take one last leap.

"You couldn't let everybody know about how you'd finally exacted your revenge. But if you did it this way, leaving your mark on some other guy's least-favorite human, nobody would know. It would be like your own private joke. Maybe one day, maybe in an obituary you write for yourself, you could tell the world what you and David Biggio did, how you had the last laugh on those goddamn lawyers."

Chopper says he has to take a piss. I tell him to make it fast, because the cops will be coming shortly to ask him a few questions. I look at my watch. It's 10:10. I hope L.D. took my request to be here at 10:30 seriously.

Chopper's been gone five minutes when I start to get concerned. What if he's taken a powder? Hell, it shouldn't matter. He's not likely going to get very far at this point.

Nothing I've told the man is going to get him convicted, but if you add it all up, the cops should be able to fill in the rest of the blanks. The longer Chopper's in the head, the longer I'm thinking this crazy scenario I've come up with is what actually happened.

Finally I get up and go back to the bathroom. The ladies' and gents' are on the other side of a plywood door that's closed. I walk through. "Gulls" is on the right. "Buoys" is on the left. To the rear is a door leading to the outside.

As I open the appropriate door, I don't see Chopper. There's only one urinal and a toilet with the door off. I wonder if Ware has left the building.

I step inside. Then I feel the metal on the back of my head.

"If you make one goddamn sound, I will splatter your fucking head all over this bathroom wall," the voice from behind me says.

Chopper Ware sounds like a man who doesn't have a lot left to lose.

CHAPTER NINETEEN

Chopper walks me out of the john, then directs me, by pushing his big-ass gun into the back of my head, to turn left and go through the back door. I hope the waitress won't mind us skipping out on the bill.

Coming back to the bathrooms to look for Mr. Ware probably wasn't the wisest thing I could have done, but "wise" isn't always at the top of my skill set. Now with the door between the toilets and the front of the restaurant closed, it's just me and a guy with a gun. I could yell for help, but I have the feeling that Chopper is very willing to pull the trigger and let the chips and my brains fall where they may.

He pushes me out the door into an empty parking lot. The hardware company van is where I spotted it earlier. I realize that a person walking out the front door of the diner wouldn't likely see it or us.

Chopper tells me to put my hands behind my back. When I try to reason with him, he strikes me with the butt of the gun, bringing me to my knees and almost knocking me out. He grabs my hands and, before I can recover, he's cuffed me.

When I cry out, he stuffs a rag in my mouth and yanks me back up.

"I was worried that you might know a little bit too much, genius, so I came prepared," he says. "It's always good to be prepared, don't you think? I figured if I waited in the john long enough, you'd come snooping."

It's closing in on ten thirty on a Monday morning, a bright, sunshiny day in this postcard-perfect little town. I'm thinking this can't be happening, but it is. There's nobody else in the parking lot as he frog-marches me to the van, keeping that gun pressed to my head. He shoves the passenger-side door open and pushes me in.

The windows are tinted, so I'm guessing it's unlikely that someone outside can see me there, gagged and cuffed. He comes around, gets in, and locks the doors.

"Let's go for a little ride," he says.

He turns south, toward the Norris Bridge. Before long we're back on the south side of the Rappahannock, headed for Topping. Soon he's turning into the long drive leading to that house he bought back in 2000, when he stopped being James Patton.

Before he leads me inside the rental house where David Biggio resided the last few years of his troubled life, he reaches into the glove compartment and comes up with some shackles for my legs. I am not feeling too optimistic about the future right now. All of a sudden, being cut to thirty hours a week seems like a relatively minor setback.

He pushes me toward the front door. I stumble a couple of times. He encourages me to get back up with that same oversized gun.

Once inside, he closes the blinds. He more or less throws me down on a ratty sofa that smells like sweat.

He pulls up a chair and straddles it, his tree-trunk legs wrapping around it like a pair of anacondas. He points the gun at me.

"So you think you've got it all figured out, I guess. But you probably didn't figure on this, did you?

"If I take that gag out, you've got to promise not to scream, or I will shoot you. There's nobody within a couple of hundred yards of here, but I'd still have to shoot you, just on principle. A man's got to have principles, don't you think?"

I nod my head and he removes the gag.

"Now then," he says, "there must be a question or two you'd like to ask me. Might be the last interview you ever do, so fire away."

I tell him that I think he's pretty much answered all my questions. Since it isn't likely that our readers are going to be privy to whatever Chopper tells me, my thirst for knowledge is far from unquenchable.

Still I would like to keep him talking. I'm afraid that what follows the talking won't be very pleasant. I'm trying to remember if the life-insurance policy the paper still springs for pays double indemnity if you get killed on the job.

Somewhere in the Kilmarnock-Topping area, there should be some Richmond cops about now. Too bad I didn't give them Chopper's home address.

How, I ask my captor, did you manage to set it up?

Chopper leans forward a bit more, so close I can smell his coffee breath.

"I thought you'd never ask."

He lays it out for me. I guess he's happy to tell this story, one that I'm pretty sure only one other person, now incinerated, has ever heard.

"I didn't really start out to do all this," he says. "For a long time, I figured that I'd just have to live the rest of my life with this big knot in my chest that all the lawsuits in the world wouldn't dissolve."

He took the money he got in the wrongful-death settlement and decided to start over. With his only child dead, his estranged wife a suicide, and not much else in the way of even distant family, he says he just wanted to make a fresh start somewhere else.

"I could of gone anywhere. Maybe I should of gone farther from Richmond. But Virginia's all I know. Somehow I couldn't see moving to Oregon or Canada or Timbuktu."

He says it wasn't that hard to get a new identity. Before his life exploded, he had worked with prisoners, part of a project his church encouraged. One of them, in for forgery, could do some amazing work.

He'd been paroled six months when James Patton approached him.

"He was an OK guy, just made bad choices. I liked him. He said I was about the only friend he had. So I told him I wanted a new life. He was able, somehow, to lay hands on a dead guy's Social Security number, and once I had the card, the rest of it was pretty easy."

Ware laughs.

"To say it like my old church might have, I was born again."

As James Ware, he says he settled on the Topping area because he knew a guy who once lived there who used to invite him down to go fishing.

"It seemed nice, like a good place to start over."

He let his beard grow, took to wearing glasses he didn't need and a big hat everywhere, and more or less buried James Patton alongside his wife and daughter.

He bought the old hardware store because he'd always liked tinkering.

"Probably should have done something like that all along," he says. "Better late than never."

He asks me if I want some water. He brings me a glass and holds it to my lips. I wonder if it'll be my last drink.

Between 2000 and 2009, James Ware became known first as Jimmy and then as Chopper. His store thrived despite a Lowe's that sprung up a half-mile away. He had a couple of girlfriends, but he dropped them when they wanted to get serious.

"I kind of liked being a man of mystery," he says.

He says the past never really was behind him, but he was able to put it aside much of the time.

"Still when I'd wake up in the morning, it'd always be there. The sun would be shining, the birds would be singing, and then I'd remember who I was and what had happened."

Despite all that, Chopper says he probably would have just "let sleeping dogs lie" back in Richmond.

"And then Biggio showed up."

He gets up and stretches. He walks around the room a little, occasionally waving his arms, one of which has a loaded gun at the end of it, for emphasis.

"What I told you about him was pretty much the truth. He was like a lost puppy when he showed up here that fall."

The winter of 2009-2010, the state was hit with about as much snow as we ever get down here. In Topping, Chopper Ware would occasionally take pity on his new tenant and invite him to the big house for a drink or two.

"He had his problems. Sometimes you could just tell that he either hadn't taken his meds or they just weren't working. But he managed to maintain most of the time."

Eventually David Biggio told the former James Patton his sad story.

"It was incredible," Chopper says. "I finally found somebody that hated lawyers almost as much as I did. They had let my daughter's killer more or less walk, and they had stolen his little girl from him."

They exchanged their grievances, probably nourishing them with bourbon.

"Somehow talking with David brought it all back to the surface. I hated the damn lawyers more than I hated the drunk kid who killed Susanna and might as well have killed Dottie. And here was a fella who felt the same way I did."

For years the two of them would talk about what they'd like to do to "those damn shysters," but Chopper says it was mostly just pipe dreams. But at some point, he came to believe that it was more than just coincidence that David Biggio had showed up on his doorstep.

"I was a churchgoer, but then I quit after the accident and the trial. It was like I had lost my faith along with everything else. I know the story of Job and all that, but I didn't have it in me to forgive God and even think there was one anymore, or at least one that gave a shit.

"But then I started thinking that maybe David Biggio didn't just stumble in here, that he was sent. You know, sent, with a capital S."

I am starting to lose whatever hope I have. It is becoming evident to me that Chopper Ware has gone beyond the point where reasoning is going to hold much sway.

"Maybe," he says, "there is a God after all, and maybe he's a God who values justice more than mercy, none of that turning-the-other-cheek bullshit. Maybe the Old Testament guy is calling the shots. An eye for a fucking eye.

"Otherwise how could the plan have come to me so clear? I woke up one morning, and there it was in my head, like somebody had planted it there."

Chopper's vision, or whatever the hell it was, came a few days after David Biggio tried to kill himself last October.

"I found him over there one night. He usually came to the big house to have a drink with me about eight or so, if he was off work. I could see the light on over there, so I went over about nine thirty to see if everything was OK."

He found Biggio about half dead from an overdose. He says he didn't call the hospital but managed to rouse his tenant eventually with black coffee and lots of walking and talking.

"He said he just couldn't do it any longer. He said he knew he was never going to be anything but a broken vessel. That's how he put it: a broken vessel. He said he was just tired of getting up every day. The pills he was supposed to take, the ones that kept the crazy away, made him feel like he was walking through molasses, he said. And when he didn't take them, it was worse."

When he finally pulled through, he thanked Ware for saving his life, but he said he wasn't sure why he did it.

"A couple of mornings later, though, when I woke up, I knew why I saved him, and what I'd saved him for. It was for me and him to get us some justice."

Adding to Chopper's conviction that he was touched by destiny was something he'd seen in our paper that week. He still subscribed to it. I guess he still wanted to know what was going on in the world he'd left.

Two days before Biggio tried to off himself, Ware saw a feature on our business pages. It was about BB&B. That august firm was celebrating its seventy-fifth anniversary. The story mentioned the fact that the partners and others in the firm had for years gotten together for happy hour on Fridays. It mentioned the present venue for those gatherings: Dark Star.

And so Chopper invited his tenant over for a little chat. He laid out his plan. He says he didn't feel bad about Biggio, who probably was going to kill himself anyhow. It was just a matter of time.

"I had this vision," Ware says, "of a bunch of lawyers all being destroyed, like when Samson brought down the temple on his enemies."

He and Biggio had flying in common. He'd even let Biggio take over the controls and finally allowed him to take his plane up by himself a couple of times.

"He was a good pilot, when his head was on straight. I knew he could do what had to be done."

Chopper says Biggio had to be talked into it a little at a time. It sure as hell didn't hurt that Ware was going to treat him to a half-million-dollar life-insurance policy, with his lost little girl as the beneficiary.

"I didn't know if she'd be able to cash in or not, if it looked like suicide, but it did sweeten the pot a little for him."

From what Chopper says, Biggio might have wanted to do harm to Stonewall Jackson Bonesteel even more than Ware wanted a piece of BB&B. Finally Chopper says his tenant agreed to do it. You do mine, and I'll do yours.

"No links, nothing to tie me to Bonesteel or Biggio to BB&B. I told him I'd go first, and then he'd pay me back."

It took a bit of planning, mostly on Chopper's part.

"I had to wear a bunch of silly-ass disguises, in case somebody recognized me. But I went to that place a couple of times on Fridays, and all those smug-ass lawyers were there, just like your paper said they would be."

He also did the legwork on Bonesteel. He says he went down to Richmond three times before he finally found a night that worked.

"It wasn't that hard, once I found out he lived alone and was supposed to be on vacation. Big old house with a big yard and lots of trees to keep the neighbors from seeing what was going on there," he says. "I'm pretty good with tools, all kinds of tools."

There was a parallel street that ran a quarter-mile behind Bonesteel's place. Chopper parked his car in the woods, slipped into the house during the day, and waited.

"He was a pretty easy mark. He drinks right much, and he was half-wasted when I finally made my move."

I note that Chopper didn't just kill him. He seemed to have made him suffer a hell of a lot before he died.

Chopper grins.

"Well," he says, "Biggio was doing me a big damn favor, and he was going to die in the process. I figured the least I could do was to give him full measure."

Carving his daughter's initials on the man, he says, was a spur-of-the-moment thing, "my little joke."

"But I made sure that he knew why he was going to die. That seemed important to Biggio."

He says he called Biggio that night, then gave him the full account of what had transpired the next day, Wednesday, and then told him it was his turn.

Chopper shakes his head.

"I probably should of just stayed the hell out here," he says. "There wasn't any need to go back. Just wait to hear about it on the six o'clock news. But I wanted to make sure it got done right, that everything was in place."

The Thursday before the big event, he and Biggio flew to Richmond. From the air, he showed Biggio the building where Dark Star did business.

Then the next day, he drove to Richmond one more time. He didn't bother wearing a disguise this time, because he figured he wouldn't be at Dark Star long enough for anybody to recognize him.

He bought the throwaway cell phone across the street about two and then he says he just drove around a little, even went by the old house where he'd spent the last twenty-five years of his previous life.

He trusted that Biggio would do everything the way they'd planned it.

"It was kind of a stretch, considering how loopy he could be sometimes."

On this particular day, as luck would have it, David Biggio must have had his meds dialed in just right.

"I drove back to that place, to the Devil's Triangle, and I parked the car on the street. About five fifteen, I slipped inside that joint and saw them all there, bellied up at the bar. They were loud, the way lawyers are. They acted like they owned the goddamn place."

So he went back outside after a few seconds. He called Biggio on his cell phone.

"All I told him was, 'Do it.'

"He didn't say nothing, just hung up. And then he did it."

Chopper says he could hear the plane coming in low off in the distance when he was getting back into his car.

"I wanted to be there to watch," he says, "but I thought that might not be such a great idea."

He says he was already on the Boulevard, headed south toward the Virginia Museum with the window open, when he heard David Biggio's final act.

"I did a U-turn down at Grove," he says. "By the time I drove back by, the flames were high enough I could see 'em from where I was driving, probably half a mile away."

He didn't know the full extent of the little hell he'd created until he got back to Topping and turned on the TV to one of the Richmond stations.

"I watched for I don't know how long. I think they scrapped some of their regular shows and kept on yapping about what a tragedy it was.

"That night, I slept as good as I've slept the last nineteen years."

I ask him if he doesn't feel just the tiniest bit bad that Biggio managed to kill and maim a lot of folks who had never gone to law school.

He shrugs his shoulders.

"Collateral damage."

His only concession to human feelings was to say that he hoped Biggio didn't suffer much. How touching.

"You reach a point," he says, "where you just don't give a shit, you know? I'm like them ISIS bastards. No turning back. No regrets."

It occurs to me that those poor sons of bitches at Dark Star were the victims of terrorists after all, even if David Biggio wasn't looking forward to the favors of seventy-two virgins.

I tell Chopper about Kate's now-late husband and the wife and little girl he's left behind.

"Well," he says, "you probably ought to thank me then, for taking out the fella that stole your wife from you."

It probably isn't worth telling Chopper Ware that it wasn't exactly like that. I think he's more into monologue than dialogue right now. I would love to have a fair shot at wiping that smile off his face though.

Chopper looks at his watch.

"I need to be getting back to the store," he says. "They're gonna think I've skipped town or something." Like we've just been having a nice chat about fishing or the weather.

He stands and motions with his gun.

"Get up."

I'm trying to save those few grains of sand still left in my personal hourglass.

"One last question."

"Make it quick."

"If you hated those lawyers so much, you must have really hated the guy who killed your daughter. Why didn't you go after him?"

He stares at me.

"You might as well know," he says at last. "He's next. The fun's just beginning."

He explains that the boy, now pushing forty, is a businessman in Chicago.

As with the BB&B attorneys, Chopper hadn't really considered doing mortal damage to the man who killed his daughter until he and Biggio got together, "although I had managed to keep up with him with the Internet and all. I've known where he lived for some time."

He scratches his back with the gun.

"Now, though, I've decided to take care of his ass too. In for a dime, in for a dollar."

Chopper's planning to take a little vacation next week. His ostensible drive over to Nashville is going to take him a bit farther north.

"Don't know if I can manage it or not," he says, "but I'm feeling pretty lucky right now."

He checks his watch again.

"OK, enough bullshit," he says. "Time to go."

He stuffs the gag back in my mouth and jerks me up.

He explains that he has a shed down by the water, near where he keeps his boat. He figures that he can shoot me there, come back around sundown and load me onto his boat, weigh me down, and turn me into crab bait somewhere out in the Chesapeake.

I think about the last time I was out on the bay, delivering Les Hacker's ashes to the sea. This is one burial at sea I would like very much to miss.

I can't even plead my case any longer, being gagged and all. I can't tell him that the cops are bound to be looking for me right now, since they've no doubt found my car in the diner's parking lot. Damn, I should have lied to him and told him I had given the Richmond cops his address.

I seem to be on the brink of paying the price for keeping what I know too close to the vest.

He's walking me toward the front door. It's going kind of slow, with me shuffling along in my shackles, not exactly in a hurry to go anywhere right now.

We are at the front door of the late David Biggio's little shack when I hear the car come to a stop in the sand outside the big house.

"Goddammit," Chopper mutters.

I look through the window. The car's occupant gets out and knocks on the front door of Chopper's house. Then she knocks again. She doesn't have the wig on now.

Keep going, I pray. Turn around and go back.

But then she looks over and she notices Chopper's big truck parked down here. She starts walking toward it, and us.

"Well, shit," my captor says, "you just seem to bring trouble with you wherever you go. You're a damn grief magnet."

I try to warn her by throwing myself against the front door. That only succeeds in earning me another blow upside the head and letting her know that there is indeed someone inside the shack.

I realize, as Sarah Goodnight approaches the front door, that there are worse things in this life than getting your own ass killed.

CHAPTER TWENTY

Sarah knocks once, waits, then tries again. Finally Ware comes to the door.

"I know he's in here," I hear her call out. I don't know if Chopper thought he could talk her away from the front door or not. Maybe he didn't want to kill her. We'll never know.

Sarah is not easily dissuaded, as I could have told my captor.

"I know you've got Willie Black somewhere around here," she says. "You're in enough trouble without doing anything else. The cops are on their way."

He doesn't seem fazed by this.

When he opens the door, he grabs Sarah's arm and tries to yank her inside.

Then she does something I really didn't expect.

She jerks away from him and pulls a gun. Where the fuck, I want to ask Sarah, did you get that thing? It isn't much. It's maybe half a foot long. I think it's what they call a Ladysmith.

She backs away and holds it with both hands. She acts like she's used a weapon before.

Chopper just shakes his head.

"What's a pretty girl like you doing with a toy like that?" he says.

He levels his own piece, which looks like you could fit the barrel of the Ladysmith inside it. Sarah hesitates.

I'm watching this from the floor. If Sarah hasn't done anything else, she's gotten his attention away from me.

I don't really have time to wait and see whether Chopper is going to order her to drop the gun or just put a big hole in her lovely chest without any conversation.

I manage to roll myself sideways, somehow lifting enough to hit Chopper in the back of his legs and making him pitch forward. There are three concrete steps leading into the cabin. He does a header down all three.

Lying on the floor and looking down, I see that he and his gun have become at least temporarily separated.

Kick the gun away, I try to scream through the gag. Kick the fucking gun away.

She probably doesn't need my direction. Sarah's a smart girl. She's jumped off the steps and into the yard to keep Chopper from falling on her and squashing her. She keeps her balance and moves quick as a bunny to where she can boot the gun farther away from its owner, who is only pissed off rather than seriously hurt by his fall.

Chopper Ware is crawling toward his gun, now maybe six feet away, when Sarah shoots him. Twice.

I'm on my stomach now, still inside the cabin. She gets him in the shoulder with the first shot and in the back with the second one. He gives out a little grunt and then lies still.

Sarah seems frozen. Then she picks up Chopper's big gun and flings it into the woods, probably thirty feet away.

She seems to notice me for the first time. She runs up the steps and takes the gag out of my mouth and helps me to my feet. She's still holding the Ladysmith. When I can talk, I ask her to please turn it away from me.

"How the hell . . . ?" I start asking.

"You think you can have all the fun," she says.

She followed me. She knew I was meeting Chopper at the diner. She even knew what time.

"You can't get away from me that easily," she says. "It really pissed me off when you wouldn't let me come with you.

"There's going to be a double byline on this one."

The wig and the floppy hat were leftovers from the last Halloween party.

"I just wanted to make sure you were in there," she says. "You have a habit of getting yourself into crap that you can't get out of."

She waited in her car, but Chopper, when he abducted me, went out the back entrance.

"When you didn't come out for a while, I went back inside. And you were gone. You really are a dumbass, Willie."

She says she remembered the way to Chopper's place and figured I might be there.

"That guy could have killed you," she says.

"Killed me? He was drawing a bead on you, as I recall."

"Well, it's your fault. I wouldn't have come here if you hadn't been such a damn chauvinist. You think a delicate little flower like me shouldn't be risking my safety, that I should leave it all to you big, strong men."

I ask her when she thinks the cops will finally get here.

"Cops? Oh, I was just bluffing him, or trying to."

"You didn't see any cops at the diner, before you left?"

She stops and ponders for a moment.

"Well I did meet a couple of cars when I was coming out here to save your butt. They looked like they were in a hurry, blue lights, sirens, the whole works."

So Sarah didn't know that L.D. Jones had the Richmond police dispatched to the diner, and L.D. and his minions don't know that I'm at Chopper Ware's estate. Great timing.

I explain that to Sarah.

"Well," she says, "if you'd talk to me once in a while, it would save us a whole lot of trouble."

I think I've heard that before somewhere.

"We're even now," Sarah informs me.

"How so?"

"For that thing in the lobby, at the newspaper. Where you tackled me when that guy was waving the gun around?"

Oh, yeah. It's been more than a year since Shorty Cole tried to hold the paper hostage and I pushed Sarah out of harm's way when she attempted to walk up and interview him and his loaded gun.

I protest that it's not quite clear who saved who today.

"Who saved 'whom,'" she corrects me. She then points out, most correctly, that, when she arrived, I was bound and gagged by a man who meant to kill me.

"Wouldn't have done you much good to knock him out the door if I hadn't been here to shoot him."

I concede that we are, indeed, even.

I ask her where the hell she got the gun. Like most sane people, she thinks the country has gone just a tad batshit about weapons. Finding out she has one, and has taken some gun-safety lessons, is a shock.

Glenn Walker, my first wife's current husband, gave me a little peashooter a few years back when it looked like I might need one. I wound up throwing it in the river, figuring I'd be as likely to shoot myself as some theoretical armed intruder.

Even at today's little party, I doubt I'd have been much good if I'd been armed. Chopper took me by surprise.

I have to admit, though, that I have no problems with Sarah packing. Not today.

She says somebody broke into one of her neighbors' apartments two months ago, while the neighbor was inside. He was lucky that the robber took his money and left without bothering to shoot him.

"But I figured, why take a chance?"

I've kind of forgotten about Chopper, out there in the yard.

"Do you think we ought to call 911?"

"I don't care if the son of a bitch bleeds to death," Sarah says, uncharitably.

And then we hear the truck start up.

We turn to see an amazing sight.

Chopper Ware has somehow, with bullets in his arm and back, managed to rouse himself and crawl to his truck, drag himself into it, and start the engine. I guess we're lucky Sarah threw the gun far enough into the woods that he figured he couldn't find it.

He guns the engine, and his oversized ride lurches forward. For a minute, I think he's going to home in on the little cabin and ram us. He could probably bring this shack down with that monster truck of his.

Instead he turns down the lane that leads to the paved road.

I'm still cuffed and shackled. Sarah helps me down the steps, then runs and gets the car. Before she leaves, she dials 911 and wedges her iPhone between my neck and shoulder.

I'm explaining the whole thing to a dispatcher who seems to be a little on the dubious side when Sarah brings the car around. Then she takes the phone and further enlightens him while she leads me around to the passenger's side.

We're a good two minutes behind Chopper by the time we get to the highway. He could have gone south on Route 3, or he could have headed back north toward the bridge leading to Kilmarnock. Sarah guesses north.

We are on the bridge when we see the brake lights up ahead. Cars are already backed up about twenty deep. In the distance, I can see a clump of people gathered on the edge of the bridge on the right-hand side.

We must make quite a sight. Sarah's leading me along the side of the stopped line of cars like I'm her prisoner. With me shuffling along, it takes us forever to get to the place where everyone's gathered.

The hole that's been knocked in the side of the bridge is just wide enough for an oversized truck to pass through. People are looking down below.

He must have waited to make that hard right turn until he was sure the water was deep enough. We can see the top of the truck bobbing in the Rappahannock. While we watch, it sinks.

In the distance, we hear sirens. In less than a minute, the blue and red lights start arriving. Near the front of the pack are two cars with City of Richmond on the side of them.

L.D. Jones jumps out of the first one. He's looking down into the river when I shuffle up behind him.

"Do you know anything about getting somebody out of handcuffs?" I ask him.

He turns and looks like he's seen a ghost.

"Goddammit, Willie. I figured you were down there. Where the hell did you disappear to?"

"Are you glad to see me, L.D.?"

He spits into the river and gives me the stink eye.

"Don't get carried away."

CHAPTER TWENTY-ONE

May 14

The coliseum has served our city well for many years, but it's about ten years past expiration date. It tends to draw things like the circus, indoor football, and midget-car racing, plus the occasional concert.

The last time I was here, if memory serves, was for a basketball game between the University of Virginia and Michigan State. We still had a minor-league ice hockey team at the time, and there was a sheet of ice underneath the basketball court. A barrier was supposed to keep moisture from rising up. It didn't. Long story short, they had to call a nationally televised game early in the second half because the players kept falling on their butts. Then the pissed-off suburbanites who'd parked in the decks near the coliseum found out that the folks who were supposed to let them back out of the decks were AWOL.

It was not one of Richmond's finest hours.

Today, though, I am happy as a pig in shit to be sitting in our antiquated sports palace.

It is, praise be to Jesus, graduation day.

At the ripe old age of twenty-seven, my delinquent daughter is finally going to commence with the rest of her life. And I can dispense with writing tuition checks to VCU.

What she will do with a degree in sociology is beyond me. She's changed majors a time or six. But reaching this point, especially with a nearly two-year-old in tow, has been a hard slog. Yeah, she made it harder on herself and me by being a knucklehead, but who among us hasn't been young and stupid? If nothing else, she'll be one of the best-educated bartender-waitresses in town.

It's a double for me. Today also is graduation day for the lovely Cindy Peroni. Like Andi, she's gone for the big bucks by picking a major guaranteed to bring a six-figure salary. In her case, English. But she already has a teaching job lined up for the fall, in one of our more benighted outlying counties.

The gang's all here. Peggy is keeping young William more or less entertained. She has now gotten to see two consecutive generations of the Black family finish college. Peggy, who didn't finish high school, couldn't be prouder if her granddaughter was Phi Beta Kappa. Of course she's a tad stoned, which might have altered her mood for the better.

She is accompanied by the equally impaired Awesome Dude. Awesome has a soft spot in his heart for VCU, since he wasted a year or so there before deciding to take the road less traveled, one that led him to skid row until Peggy provided him a roof for his muddled head.

And sitting next to Andi is Walter McGinness, who seems to be a keeper, at least according to Andi. He doesn't appear to be bothered by the fact that my daughter comes with the aforementioned William who, though adorable, is another man's child.

I spend as much time as I can getting everyone settled before returning to Cindy, whose only other guest is her son. I've had the chance to spend a little time with Chip, who works with his real-estate developer father, from whom Cindy split when her son was still in high school. He is on tenuous terms with his mom. Understandably, he is on even more tenuous terms with me.

Despite the stoned and the snippy, I'm pleased as punch to be here.

It has been a somewhat crazy three weeks, even by my standards.

The concussion's aftereffects went away in a couple of days, but I did have to dictate my part of the story to Sarah Goodnight, who definitely earned her part of the double byline. I hear about all these NFL players who have permanent and horrible brain damage from too many blows to the head. I might be the first newspaperman to suffer from CTE. For some reason, a variety of people over the years have tried to use my noggin as a piñata.

We didn't print much in the Tuesday paper, since I spent Monday night in the local hospital in Kilmarnock and Sarah didn't know the whole story.

What ran Tuesday was mostly a story about the apparent suicide of the guy whose plane crashed into Dark Star. It left many more questions than answers.

L.D. Jones actually did us a favor by not revealing to the news media in general that Chopper Ware also had been shot twice before doing a swan dive into the Rappahannock River, or that he had earned those two bullet wounds by abducting a dues-paying member of the Fourth Estate. Sarah was grilled a bit more than she should have been, but the gun she used to shoot his ass was registered, and the cops determined finally that she had a very good reason to use it. And they'll probably figure that it was drowning rather than gunshot wounds that did Chopper in.

Wednesday's stories, though, were lulus. In our version, the police were tipped off about Ware's possible involvement in the Dark Star massacre when an alert flatfoot (our Gillespie) went back and took a closer look at the tapes the cops seized from the 7-Eleven. They were already in Kilmarnock, ready to detain Chopper, when their suspect drove his truck off the Norris Bridge and into the Rappahannock.

The chief was quoted as saying that the police had strong evidence that the suspect had "enticed" David Biggio into crashing his plane and killing two dozen people. Again there would have been more questions than answers if there hadn't been another piece, in which Sarah did the writing while I dictated my part and we argued over commas and semicolons. When I had to insert myself into the story, I was "one of this newspaper's reporters." As a guy who hates reporters who plant their asses right in the middle of what they're writing, I feel like a damn hypocrite, but this seemed like the best way to do it.

So we laid it out for our breathless readers. And we knew they would be breathless. Wheelie and Rita Dominick even signed off on bumping up our city edition run by 10,000 copies, because by then the whole town was buzzing about what really happened on April 8. Actually it isn't that hard to get Wheelie and the publisher to sign off on just about anything these days. She's already gotten her next assignment, and Wheelie was wearing out the copier sending out résumés, being somewhat short of sure about his future with our new corporate masters.

It was easier for us to write because Biggio and Ware have gone on to their rewards, or punishments. The dead can't sue.

It started like this: "Sometime before dawn on April 6, a man killed and mutilated one of Richmond's most prominent lawyers in the lawyer's own home. The killer had never met the man he slaughtered. He was only carrying out his part of a bargain.

"Two days later, when a tortured soul crashed an airplane into a crowded eatery and took the lives of twenty-five innocent strangers, the unholy pact was completed."

OK, so maybe Chopper Ware might say some of those lawyers weren't innocents. Too bad, Chopper. You can tell your version of the story in hell.

We walked the readers through what Ware told me, from the time he and Biggio met until his diseased brain hatched the plot. It points out all the grievances both men had against various members of the legal profession.

It brings in the life-insurance policy, Biggio's reward for going along with Ware's plan, plus the fact that the policy is almost certainly not going to enrich either young Brandy or her mother and shiftless stepfather.

We had to do a little fancy dancing with the 7-Eleven tapes. We had to give credit to the donut-addicted Gillespie for going back and taking a second look at the tapes, going far enough to discover Chopper Ware buying a throwaway cell phone and then driving away the day of the murders. It was the only way to save Peachy Love's lovely ass. This time, she sent me roses.

L.D. Jones might suspect that Gillespie isn't usually the sort to break a major case, but he can't argue with the facts. Gillespie, never a man for the grand gesture, sends me a dozen maple donuts from Sugar Shack.

It's a good day when your sources are thanking you.

MediaWorld surprised all of us, most especially Wheelie, by keeping him on as managing editor. He was all set to take a job in Wichita or Tulsa or some godforsaken place when he got the news. We were all glad for him. Better the editor you know than the one some soulless entity brings in.

Most amazingly, they turned the money faucet on just a bit. Raindrops of mercy fell especially on me, because the new suits decided to take everybody who had been cut to thirty hours back up to forty. In lieu of an actual raise, this feels like one.

It looks like Cindy and I will be able to continue our luxurious lifestyle at the Prestwould for a while, at least until Kate decides to sell the unit.

Kate has gone back to work, as I thought she would. She doesn't give up easily. Hell, it took her years to give up on me. She seems to have found some small solace in knowing the "why" of how her husband died, even if it didn't make much sense.

"Greg was in junior high when this guy's daughter was killed," she said when she'd heard and read the whole story.

There wasn't much use in trying to explain crazy. At some point, either a God with a very strange sense of humor or plain bad luck threw together two men who might have swallowed their losses and their bile and moved on. We are lucky, I guess, with all the free-floating insanity around us, that it doesn't happen more often than it does.

It always bothers me that we wind up writing about the bad guys instead of their victims. Some bastard was selling T-shirts within two days of our big story with Chopper Ware's visage on the front and the words "Revenge is a bitch." Sarah and I have started doing a series of stories on the victims' families and how they're coping, but I know they'll get about a tenth the readership that Chopper and David's big adventure got. If people really wanted news about good people instead of bastards, that's what we'd give them on a regular basis.

I don't think Kate and Marcus Green will be able to do much for Brandy Klassen and her parents. The life-insurance policy is toast. Bobby in particular seems to blame me personally for telling the world just how obviously insane and suicidal David Biggio was when he did the deed and made the Devil's Triangle live up to its long-ago sobriquet. Bobby has called me a couple of times to tell me how I've fucked up his fucked-up life. He threatened to kick my ass next time he has the chance. I told him to take a number, but asked him if he'd mind waiting until I recovered from my last ass-kicking.

As for Cindy, well, she was a little miffed that I'd put myself in harm's way without telling her anything about what that last trip to Topping might entail.

"I might've been waving good-bye to you for the last time," she said when she got to the hospital that day. "How the hell am I supposed to live like that? When are you going to pull some stunt like this again? There's bound to be a next time."

I promise her that I won't, that I'm getting too old for this crap. But she and I both know it's bullshit. They'd have to chain me to a desk to make me come inside and stop sticking my nose into other people's business. I wouldn't last five minutes.

She seems to have forgiven me for not sharing though. She has done some kind of interior accounting and figured that the pluses outweigh the minuses of Willie World.

I'm not at all sure she's right. When we were back in our own bed in the Prestwould, me with a big bandage around my head, I asked her what in the hell kept her from leaving my ass.

"I don't have any better prospects at the present," she said. "Plus, I feel sorry for you."

I think she was kidding. But, hell, I'll play the sympathy card if that's what it takes to keep her.

The commencement comes and, finally, goes. The damn thing lasts forever. I asked both Andi and Cindy if they couldn't just have VCU mail them their sheepskins. I think I was still sleeping off a hangover when my class walked down the aisle. They both seem more sentimental than I had realized.

And so I stand here, pleased and blessed, as pictures are taken and kisses are exchanged. Things don't always work out, but sometimes, if you keep throwing stuff against the wall, something sticks.

Cindy reaches over and takes my left hand in her right one as she accepts congratulations from friends. When she rubs the gold band adorning my ring finger, where three others previously resided, I pray for a bond that will hold forever.

Maybe, as my esteemed best man Abe Custalow said, the fourth time will be a charm.

Willie Black is not afraid of commitment.